THE DIE IS CAST

THE DIE IS CAST

ROBERT DESNOS

TRANSLATED BY JESSE L. ANDERSON

WAKEFIELD PRESS / CAMBRIDGE, MASSACHUSETTS

Wakefield Press, P.O. Box 425645, Cambridge, MA 02142

Originally published as *Le vin est tiré . . .* by Éditions Gallimard in 1943.

Cover image: Man Ray, *Emak-Bakia*, 1926 (film still)

This book was set in Garamond Premier Pro and Helvetica Neue Pro by Wakefield Press. Printed and bound by McNaughton & Gunn, Inc., in the United States of America.

ISBN: 978-1-939663-69-6

Available through D.A.P./Distributed Art Publishers
75 Broad Street, Suite 630
New York, New York 10004
Tel: (212) 627-1999
Fax: (212) 627-9484

1 2 3 4 5 6 7 8 9 10

CONTENTS

TRANSLATOR'S INTRODUCTION

To readers familiar with the more celebrated selections from Robert Desnos's oeuvre, his late novel *The Die Is Cast* (*Le vin est tiré . . .*[1]) will look something like an oddity, a blip of social fiction toward the end of a somewhat irregular output of surrealist poetry. And this impression wouldn't be wrong: the book—which tracks the deterioration of a small band of Parisian opium addicts—is indeed an oddity when set beside the rest of Desnos's literary work, not simply for being social fiction, but for being fiction without any qualifier attached. When *The Die Is Cast* was published in 1943, Desnos had written only a handful of other novels: *Liberty or Love!*, *Mourning for Mourning*, and *The Punishments of Hell*, books an anglophone hesitates to even label as novels (the French have always been more generous with the word) owing to their diminutive length and heterodox content. Add to this the fact that *The Die Is Cast* was written some two decades after these other fictional works, and the blip stands out even more.

But if we take a closer look at Desnos's work and life, the novel begins to make more sense. Desnos was socially engaged to a degree that was unusual among other early surrealists. He covered any number of political and social topics while working as a journalist in his twenties, and much of his later poetry was overtly political. And he didn't limit himself to words: during the German Occupation, he used his journalistic access to privileged information to aid the French Resistance, an action that would eventually cost him his life.

Other instances of Desnos's political convictions and development can be found throughout his biography. In 1928, he helped smuggle the Cuban writer and dissident Alejo Carpentier out of his home country aboard a France-bound ship. On another occasion, Desnos began smashing glasses in a club after a Black friend was refused admission, on racial grounds, to the dance floor. More specific to the concerns of the novel, Desnos had watched his beloved Yvonne George, a Belgian cabaret singer, succumb to opium addiction—a passive incident compared to the more engaged ones just cited, but it's also the most central to understanding the germination of *The Die Is Cast.*

The experiences and impulses necessary to write the novel, then, were there to be drawn upon. Desnos—who'd already written poems and prose, song lyrics, plays, advertisements, and radio jingles—simply had to make the decision to sit down and write it.

* * *

Robert Desnos was born on 4 July 1900, to parents on a steady rise toward the middle class. His father sold poultry in Les Halles, a famous and expansive Parisian market, and for most of Robert's childhood the family lived in the nearby Marais neighborhood, a medieval section of Paris whose mystic atmosphere Desnos would credit with spurring his precocious imagination. He was young enough to avoid fighting in the First World War but still had to complete mandatory military service after high school. It was during this time that he first met—through mutual friend Benjamin Péret—André Breton and Louis Aragon, who would soon become figureheads of the surrealist movement. It wasn't until Desnos was discharged in 1922, however, that he was fully integrated into the burgeoning group and began making a name for himself as a poet.

The most noteworthy of Desnos's early experiences with the Breton-helmed group were what are known as the automatist sessions, nocturnal séances during which those who gathered—sometimes individually, sometimes in groups—appeared to fall into a trance through a kind of self-hypnosis and then interacted with the others from an apparently heightened or altered state of awareness. How authentic these trances were is debatable, but what's clear from contemporaneous accounts is that Desnos was far more impressive than the others while hypnotized (an account of this can be found in Breton's surrealist classic, *Nadja*). He would become a seemingly endless fount of short, word play–laden poems, and some of his earliest published works, the "Rrose Sélavy" poems, were a product of these sessions.

Desnos went on composing surrealist poetry through the 1920s while also beginning his career as a journalist. This didn't sit well with Breton, who saw journalism as a profession unworthy of someone with Desnos's linguistic talents. It was an early crack in their friendship, and by the end of the decade—after many boyish internecine battles among the surrealists—Desnos had become, so to speak, unaffiliated, a free agent. Some months later, in April 1930, Desnos went through another life-shifting event: the death of Yvonne George, whom he'd fallen in love with shortly after meeting her in the mid-1920s. By many accounts, Desnos was obsessed with the Belgian chanteuse, and though his love went unrequited, he grew increasingly obsequious as her health deteriorated from the combined effects of opiate addiction and tuberculosis. During the last two years of her life, Desnos had even begun hunting down drugs for her.

So the 1930s, for Desnos, began with ruptured artistic ties and a dead love interest. He soon found replacements for both. In the creative domain, Desnos began work as a radio broadcaster, a job he adored and would continue at until the outbreak of the Second World War. Reflecting his wide-ranging curiosity, Desnos was involved with a variety of programs and hosted several, including one dedicated to the exploration of foreign cultures and another, *La Clef des Songes* (The key to dreams), in which he interpreted listeners' dreams. He also discovered a knack for marketing, and wrote radio ads for pharmaceuticals, furs, the National Lottery, chocolate, perfume, and much else besides. Unfortunately, and owing to the fact that Desnos lived in a time before widespread recording of the radio, only some twenty minutes of his voice have been passed down to posterity.

As for love, Desnos had already fallen for another woman by the time of George's death. Her name was Youki Foujita, a Frenchwoman who'd adopted her decidedly un-French first name—it was originally Lucie—after marrying Japanese painter Tsuguhara Foujita. Desnos and Youki were interested in each other while the marriage was still intact, but the sudden and lasting departure of her husband in 1931, along with his sanctioning of their relationship in a farewell letter, allowed the two to go beyond mere interest and move in together. Though never legally married, they would remain a couple until the end of Desnos's life.

He published scantily in the 1930s, but Desnos was still writing and, for a time, strove to complete a poem every night before bed. It was during this period that Desnos wrote one of his most celebrated poems, "The Tale of the Bear," a response to the interwar political upheaval in Paris and an example of his artistic engagement with society at large. It was a harbinger of the kind of work Desnos would publish in the even more turbulent decade to come.

In the fall of 1939, Desnos was mobilized and sent to Brittany with the 436th Regiment of Pioneers. Upon his return to Paris the following August, he found that the radio stations had become propaganda outlets for the Vichy regime and returned to newspaper work to make a living. His columns were often, to varying degrees of explicitness, politically charged, with pieces on themes like neighbor-on-neighbor denunciation and French unity. He also wrote regular reviews of jazz records, a poke in the eye to the Nazis, who considered the genre degenerate.

The articles weren't enough. Soon after some thirteen thousand French Jews were rounded up in, and subsequently deported from, the Velodrome d'Hiver stadium in July 1942, Desnos joined the Agir ("Act," in English) Resistance cell, for whom, in addition to supplying information gathered using his press credentials, he forged identification documents.

The Die Is Cast was released the following year by Gallimard. Employing an ensemble cast of characters to show opium's non-discretionary appeal across class and generational lines, Desnos is explicit in his preface regarding the novel's purpose: "This book attempts, without the author necessarily believing himself to have succeeded, to demonstrate that social circumstances are responsible for the daily increase in the diffusion of drugs, that addicts deserve to be brought back into the fold of daily life, that the current suppression-based laws are absurd, unjust, harmful, and that it's vital, with the assistance of the medical community, to reform our barbaric legal system." The book is antidrug, but it's not anti-addict. The empathy espoused by Desnos, in these lines written nearly eighty years ago, is admirable; the argument he makes is prescient. One need only look at the success of models that have adopted an approach similar to that described by Desnos—Portugal being a notable example—to see how clear-sighted he was.

Though it does at times take turns toward the surrealistic that are reminiscent of—and arguably even allusive to—his earlier writings, the book's straightforward aim renders fruitless the deep, symbol-driven exegesis that can be done with much of Desnos's work: *The Die Is Cast* speaks for itself.

Of course, the reader can draw connections between the text and Desnos's life. Barbara—the wealthy, elusive love interest of Antoine, the closest character the book has to a protagonist—is modeled on Yvonne George, and Antoine's continually thwarted relationship with Barbara bears more than a passing resemblance to Desnos's own doomed courtship. Antoine's visit to Barbara's apartment in the third chapter gives an idea of the utter powerlessness Desnos may have felt in his pursuit of George. To take the Antoine–Desnos connection further, the opening scene, a hallucinogenic memory of Antoine's military service in Morocco, is almost certainly based on Desnos's own posting in Morocco before he joined the surrealists. And Les Halles, where Desnos's father worked, is memorably described through Antoine's eyes in one of the book's best scenes.

But such details, in the end, are trivia. What matters is that *The Die Is Cast* is a very good book—entertaining, moving, replete with descriptions and scenes that are not easily forgotten—written by a highly and multitudinously talented writer. That Desnos hadn't written any fiction of note for fifteen years only makes his accomplishment here more impressive.

Desnos also published the poetry collection *État de veille* (which included "Tale of the Bear") in 1943; the year after, he published another set of poems in *Contrée*. Both books were political in a manner the Germans would not have appreciated, and both were semiclandestine—meaning they were available in some bookstores but had evaded the collaborationist censors. *The Die Is Cast* allowed Desnos to openly address a political issue close to his heart, without fear that it might land him in prison, or worse.

Tragically, Desnos's work in the Resistance was already leading him toward such a fate.

* * *

Desnos was arrested on 22 February 1944. A colleague from *Aujourd'hui*, the newspaper he was then working for, had called his apartment that morning to warn him that the Gestapo were out looking for him. Desnos helped Alain Brieux—a young man he'd taken in to help avoid a forced work program recently instituted by the Germans—escape and then stayed behind to protect Youki. A trio of officers soon arrived and took Desnos away to Gestapo headquarters, on rue des Saussaies. From there, Desnos passed through two transit camps and on 30 April arrived at Auschwitz-Birkenau, where he had his head shaved, was put into a striped uniform, and had the number 185,443 tattooed on his arm.

He made it out of Auschwitz. It seems that those running the camp were surprised to have been sent a non-Jewish convoy, and Desnos's group was sent away to Buchenwald in mid-May. Before the end of the month, Desnos would be transferred again, this time to Flossenbürg. It was to be another short stay—on 2 June, he left for Flöha, on the Czech border. He arrived the next day and would remain there until April.

His time at Flöha wasn't as hard as it might have been. He was able to receive packages from Youki to supplement the meager rations, and his duties were among the camp's easiest. According to fellow prisoners, he was voluble and often in surprisingly high spirits, telling stories and reading fortunes in the evening. This all changed, however, when a confrontation with a server led to Desnos throwing hot soup into the other's face. As punishment, Desnos would be given the camp's most demanding jobs for the remainder of his stay.

This would last only about a month. It was the spring of 1945, and the Americans were moving inexorably closer, leading to the camp's evacuation on 14 April. The prisoners then began a brutal march toward another camp, Terezin, or Theresienstadt, in Czechoslovakia. Conditions along the way were wretched, and Desnos was much older than most of the other prisoners. Nevertheless, he made it to Terezin alive—in bad shape, but alive—on 7 May. The Allies won the war the very next day; the prisoners were free; the only thing to be done now was find a way back home. Desnos wouldn't make it. He grew increasingly ill, and just days after meeting a Czech doctor who'd recognized him from a photo in *Nadja*, Desnos died on the morning of 8 June.

Weeks before his arrest, a film for which Desnos had written the screenplay, *Bonsoir Mesdames, Bonsoir Messieurs*, was released in Parisian cinemas. Two months into his imprisonment, two of his most celebrated works were published, *Contrée* and *Trente chantefables pour les enfants sages à chanter sur n'importe quel air*, a collection of nursery rhymes that's still taught to children today. Later this same year, *Le bain avec Andromède* would come out, and 1945 saw the publication of a play, *La Place de l'étoile*, and a long poem, "Calixto."

Desnos's arrest and deportation, it seems, cut short an unprecedented stream of productivity. We can only guess what else might have come of it.

NOTE

1. Literally, "the wine is drawn," a French expression whose English equivalents include this translation's title and "the bed is made," the message being that some actions lead to less than desirable consequences that one must face. Although the English-language idioms capture the meaning of the French, they lack the allusion to intoxication, which is especially pertinent in a book about opium addiction.

THE DIE IS CAST

PREFACE

Many well-intentioned books have been written on the world of drugs, both by addicts and by the naive. But despite themselves, the former, beginning with Thomas de Quincey, have always presented the black or white muse in a seductive manner, while the latter haven't made any effort to enter into the drama that plays out among this ill-fated group of men and women. And, most importantly, no one has ever attempted to bring the question of addiction to the plane of realism.

Why are there drug addicts?

Are addicts worth the effort that's required to help them?

Do current laws allow said help?

This book attempts, without the author necessarily believing himself to have succeeded, to demonstrate that social circumstances are responsible for the daily increase in the diffusion of drugs, that addicts deserve to be brought back into the fold of daily life, that the current suppression-based laws are absurd, unjust, harmful, and that it's vital, with the assistance of the medical community, to reform our barbaric legal system.

Drug addicts and the insane face a similar situation. More than a century after Pinel, our system of asylums still lacks a medical foundation. And neither the police nor the courts will be able to stop the progress of these poisons, poisons that, let's not forget, are no longer a privilege of the wealthy and intellectual classes, but which also now threaten the proletariat and the nation as a whole. So long as the social order victimizes the free development of the individual, men and women will continue to seek in opium and heroin illusory compensations, as well as the key to a slow suicide.

In twenty years, drug use will have spread to every level of society, perhaps even to the countryside, and by then it will be too late to stop its advance.

This book is set in Paris. But the experiences of its hapless heroes, with the exception of several details, could just as easily have taken place in any city of any country throughout the world. The author doesn't claim to have presented a French vice, but a human vice. If this vice threatens France for the same reasons it does any other nation, France is by no means the nation most at risk.

The moon shone down, its light reflecting out from the black chasms it had dug between the buildings of the camp. The air, the earth, and the night were breathing. Fragrances rose from the tussocks and the clods of dirt. The sentinels let themselves be lulled by these exhalations and by the languor of midnight, by the almost perceptible turning of the planet and by the moonlight, which softened the red of their chechias and belts to orange, gave their khakis the shine and glint of silk, and seemed to cause the barbed wire to blossom.

Several hundred meters from the camp a cluster of olive trees could be made out, or rather *the* cluster of olive trees. After sunset, after the roll call, it was a place best avoided. More than one Spahi, more than one Zouave, more than one tringlot had lost his life there after a night of debauchery. By nightfall, the gates were closed. By then, no one should have been outside . . . At the officers' canteen one could hear any number of stories about young men killed by a dissident lying in wait, and it will never be known why those four or five olive trees weren't chopped down.

Just beyond them began a steep hill, covered with vines, surrounded by hidden traps: fences, poles, string. At its top, sheltered by Saracen walls and flanked with squat, square towers, the Arab city slept. With the black night as its backdrop, the city seemed even whiter than usual; the brightness was so great, the shadows so intense, the contrast so stark, that the eye lost any notion of perspective.

A sudden noise pierced the silence, a gallop that startled the drowsy soldiers; a white horse appeared on the hill, running along the walls without a saddle, without a rider, without a harness, its mane blowing in the wind behind it. It followed the walls and then disappeared around a corner.

It was a stray horse, in search of its master, panicked by its own shadow, lost in its own world.

Several minutes went by; then the gallop could again be heard. The horse reappeared around a bend, ran past, vanished. It continued its course around the city with a mechanical regularity.

Its image and the sounds it produced were uncannily distinct, as if all at once the moon was amplifying its size, the noise of its hooves, and the resulting echo. Out here in the countryside, its presence took on tremendous significance, like the sight of a meteor or the celestial signs from ancient times.

The Senegalese Tirailleurs raised their hands to the gris-gris sewn into their chechias.

The nocturnal atmosphere then underwent a transformation. A door slammed shut. A noncommissioned officer in shirtsleeves approached, his culottes beating against his exposed calves. He yawned, lit a cigarette, and used his watch to measure the time it took the animal to complete a lap. Others came to join him.

The Black soldiers' unease had spread to the Arabs and Kabyles, and soon had penetrated the Europeans as well: boys from Paris, plowmen from Beauce, winegrowers from Burgundy. In subdued voices, they exchanged the tales of ghosts, spirits, and haunted houses that every man keeps in reserve for such evenings.

Out in the wilderness, an owl hooted. Then, close by, the yelping of a jackal could suddenly be heard, giving everyone a start and causing a prowler to curse the Christians in the names of Abd el-Kader and Abd el-Melek with a guttural roar and a series of shrieks as poignant as those produced by love.

A warrant officer took a sentry's rifle, carefully aimed, fired at the animal, missed. Others began doing the same. The gunfire resounded for a long time through the mountains. The camp's officers came to join the soldiers.

Every time the horse appeared around the bend in the wall, a salvo of shots resounded, their echoes rolling like empty barrels out toward the desert. The horse went on galloping. Like flocks of cotton drawn out from his nostrils, white clouds floated by in the sky. Then, suddenly, it was dawn.

A first ray of sunlight appeared over the mountains, struck the roofs of the city, and, without illuminating it, passed over the camp. At the same instant, the horse, mane billowing, was absorbed, dissolved by the light. The galloping ceased immediately. Birds were singing, and insects were buzzing, working their way, with intervals of silence, into their usual rhythm.

The exhausted men went back to sleep. Antoine was left alone. He took a piece of bread from the canteen's kitchen and left the camp to pick a wild dandelion and, from a nearby spring, several sprigs of watercress to eat in the morning breeze.

The sun was still gentle; the dew had almost evaporated . . .

Evening was falling over the Marne. A final boat was passing by, hurrying toward Nogent. The Rendez-Vous des Pêcheurs, which sat at a good distance from the villas and cafés, comprised six tables and three bowers that overlooked the river. Behind moss-covered walls and thick trees one could see a large house with closed windows and, separated by a lane, another estate inside a park. The April evening was quiet, cool, and aromatic. There were a dozen or so people chatting on the terrace.

"Our friend Antoine is a wonderful soul," declared Courvoisier.

"I have to say, your story frightens me . . ."

It was Barbara Durand speaking. She and Courvoisier were radiant with youth and health, even if there was already a trace of languor in their gaze and posture that gave off an impression of age, fatigue.

Beside them sat Artenac, who, despite his rustic grace and because of his robustness, looked like something of a lout. He was the one who'd brought them to Mother Lampion at the Rendez-Vous des Pêcheurs. He lived nearby in a small, isolated house situated between the two estates, where it was so quiet it seemed as if you were a hundred leagues outside the city. They knew very little about Antoine Maison, who'd just recounted one of his memories from Africa.

"Should we go in?" asked Berthe.

"To eat?"

Artenac pointed to the set table in the other room.

"A *bouillon corsé*, a poule au blanc, deep-fried gudgeons, salad, and a tart made by Mother Lampion herself."

"Are you hungry?"

"Yes, Berthe, I'm hungry."

"I'm not."

"Don't listen to her," said Courvoisier, "she's an amateur smoker. It kills her appetite. Me, on the other hand, I could smoke six pipes and then eat a wild boar. Isn't that right, Barbara?"

"Let's go in," she said in response.

The meal was festive. Courvoisier asked for coffee, decided to make it himself and serve it to his friends. An excitement had come over them while eating, and they were in a rush to finish.

"So, my young friends, are we enjoying ourselves?" asked Mother Lampion. "You're all set for the night now. I don't imagine you'll be going off to bed right away."

The end of the alley was blocked by the double door that led to Artenac's house. Behind it was a mossy courtyard, at one end of which, bringing to mind a stage set, sat the small, white, vine-covered building. Two narrow paths followed the walls of the large estates and led to a triangle-shaped garden that stretched out from the back of the house. Artenac opened a French window and everyone went in through a sitting room—a bedroom to one side—and then into another room with a view of the garden. Mattresses and blankets were piled up in a corner. In several minutes, they'd been transformed into large divans. Barbara squeezed lemons and oranges into shakers while the others set up the trays, pipes, and lamps.

"There's a quite a few of us," remarked Auportain, "and only three lamps."

"So two lamps with three people and one with four," Courvoisier proposed.

"No . . . something much simpler. I'll eat a bit of your Yunnan and wait my turn."

"My Yunnan!" protested Artenac . . . "I believe you mean Benares."

"Yunnan, my dear, and so much the better. Save your Benares for the ladies. As for myself, I prefer the contraband drug that never fails to satisfy. I prefer, that is, the vintage wine to the aperitif."

"As you wish!" And, slightly irritated, Artenac smiled . . . "I'm not going to lecture you about opium. You know much more about it than I do, big adventurer that you are."

"Have you been to the Indies?" asked Antoine.

"Yes."

"And is that where you . . . ?"

"Developed a taste for the bamboo pipe? Not at all. That happened at rue des Martyrs in Paris, twenty years after I got back. In the Indies, I drank whiskey and was better off because of it."

"Auportain is quite the character," asserted Lily. "He's always saying nasty things about opium, but he's the most dedicated smoker here."

"And the oldest . . . yes, I've smoked for twenty-five of my sixty-five years. But at least when I was your age, I had better things to do than get high."

"Oh, Doctor! You're going to ruin the whole night with your preaching."

This came from Barbara who, already stretched out, was cooking a crackling bead of opium on the end of a needle, over the lamp.

Without responding, Auportain put a dosage of opium into his glass, filled it with water, stirred it with a little spoon, and then swallowed the bitter liquid. He lit a cigarette and, taking Maison by the arm, led him out to a bench in the garden.

The sound of flapping wings could be heard coming from the trees, along with several quickly halted chirps. The pale crescent moon sent its light out over the lawn and the quivering water of a small fountain.

"What the hell are you doing here?" the old smoker asked his companion.

"Me?"

"Yes, you. You're twenty-five years old and look like you might have greater ambitions than mummifying yourself. Don't kid yourself into thinking that all this nonsense will see you through to a hundred."

"A hundred? And what would be the point of living that long?"

"Have you suffered?"

"No."

"Then what do you expect to get out of making love to a woman who acts like a young mare and forces you into a new battle each and every night? An old guy like me has no trouble seeing the effect Barbara has on you."

"Sure, Barbara's charming . . . but . . ."

"But what?"

"But what can I do about it? She's rich, I'm poor."

"Foolish young man, what does that matter?"

"It matters."

"Well then, make yourself some money."

"Easy to say."

"Easier to do than using drugs to get what you want. Do you think this stuff is cheap? If you want it, you need money, lots of money, and drugs will stop you from making it, and if you do make it you'll be tired enough in the evening to prefer sleep over opium's blissful but hollow insomnia. It's important to have some strong desire in your heart, my young friend, one that's always got a grip on you."

He raised his hand toward the sky, where a shooting star had just passed.

"Make a wish."

Maison hesitated, then finally said:

"To be loved."

"Not like that! The shooting star can't have gone out before you've made your wish. You have to be eager for what you want and scream out, 'I want the woman I love!' or, 'I want fame,' or 'I want money'; believe me, having money's better than having the pipe. And you need to want what you desire immediately, and greedily."

"But I can only approach Barbara when I'm smoking . . ."

"Then save her or save yourself."

The night was now pitch-black. Maison could only see Auportain's face when he took a drag off his cigarette, the red light illuminating his large, crow's feet-bordered eyes, his boldly delineated nose, his slender mouth, and, embellished at the cheekbones by Rosacea, his olive complexion. Courvoisier liked to say that the doctor was a man of the highest distinction. Although it was said that he'd had a brilliant and turbulent youth, after two generations the evidence of such social grandeur fades more surely than a parchment from the Middle Ages. The group knew that Dr. Auportain had been a king of Paris in the 1890s, and, retired to the depths of some province, or confined to the society of the elderly, a number of his contemporaries still remembered the names, and the names had been well known, of his mistresses. Moreover, in the bibliography of a thesis on the great epidemic illnesses, a student could still cite Auportain's "Observations on the 1886 Epidemic of Plague in Chandernagor, Mahé, and in the Province of Madras," observations that had earned him, in addition to enthusiastic interviews in the newspapers and the esteem of his peers, the Legion of Honor, which had made him the youngest legionnaire of his time. Another ten years, twenty at most, and, in the wake of his death, he would be entirely forgotten. One day, on a yellowed newspaper at the back of some attic, his name might catch the attention of someone opening up an old box. And that would be the destiny of this marvelous man, endowed with so many qualities of both heart and mind and whose clairvoyant powers made it impossible for him to deceive himself that things might be otherwise.

After a silence, he began speaking again:

"How long have you known Courvoisier?"

"Six months. Barbara introduced me to him, and to everyone else in there, for that matter. Even you."

"Did you know he has the potential to be the premier physicist of our time?"

"I knew that he was somehow involved with science. But isn't there something between him and Barbara?"

"I wouldn't know anything about that, and I couldn't care less. There you have a young fellow with looks to kill for, but who has nothing better to do than stupefy himself. You find him charming . . . But he's nothing compared to what he could be."

"What about Artenac? What's his story?"

"He's an imbecile. Wasting his time as well, that one. At his age, built like he is, I would've already crossed Brazil, tended herds in Argentina, hunted elephant in Africa, and left behind a son on every island in the Pacific. Hails from a bourgeois family, now an orphan, and rich enough to do without the whims of a young man."

"And Barbara?"

"I was waiting for you to come back to her. She's rather beautiful, isn't she? She also gets thirty thousand francs each month from her pension . . . Her father? He dedicates all his time to his business, and her mother, well, she's half-crazy, takes part in table-turning séances that last entire nights . . . something like a million jewels, on top of that, set aside in a bank . . . Many more millions to be inherited one day and such robust health that she'll have the last word of us all. One day they'll put Barbara Durand in a cemetery and her health will at last be isolated and no longer exposed to mistreatment."

"Why don't we go back in and smoke a bit more?"

"If you insist."

The two of them went back into the salon. Around one lamp sat Courvoisier, Berthe, Lily; around another, Barbara, Arichetti, Artenac. A strong, seductive, and unforgettable aroma hung in the air, streaming over the walls, permeating the curtains. It was so overpowering that Maison felt as if he were taking it in with his entire body.

Columot and Marie-Jacqueline were already nodding in a dark corner of the room, on a pile of cushions. The third tray was unoccupied. Antoine and Auportain settled down at it. The skills of the latter were extraordinary. Beneath his thin fingers the needle turned while the pellet of opium swelled, lightened in color, neared the desired state. Then, with a brisk movement, he stuck it onto the bowl, pierced it, and held out the end of the large bamboo pipe to his companion. He had deliberately chosen the simplest of the available pipes, one without adornments, without precious metals. Nothing more than a piece of bamboo with a clay bowl, a simple saddle, and an amber tip. His choice was thus a lesson in elegance for Artenac, whose ivory pipe, with its complicated adornments and earthenware bowl, was little more than an object built for exportation, and for Barbara as well, who had an antique pipe that was a veritable museum piece.

"Look at me," Auportain was saying to Maison . . . "twenty-five years of smoking has led to this: I can prepare a pipe better than almost anyone else in Europe. After this, you can laugh your heart out at the so-called dedication of stamp collectors."

Courvoisier addressed Antoine:

"Take note, my friend. The day the doctor agrees to smoke a pipe you've prepared—and on that day and that day only—you'll be able to say that you know how to smoke."

Berthe Cassotte wanted to let her opinion be known.

"You frighten me with your talk of technique. While you're eating, the cook doesn't come to tell you how he gutted and prepared the fowl, right? You ought to do the same with your art of pipe preparation."

Berthe was a pretty girl who went through life with the aloofness and insouciance of a great adventuress. Nothing surprised her except the surprise of others at her oftentimes wild behavior. Who was her father, her mother, her family? Nobody knew. It was said that she was married to a famous ambassador and was welcomed in some of London's most exclusive places. Beyond that, whoever wanted to learn more was welcome to try. For although opium often leads to an exchange of secrets, Berthe had never mentioned anything regarding her own past. Moreover, she lied with the confidence of someone who derives satisfaction from their own dishonesty and who hardly cares whether or not people believe them. And so, mixing the true with the false while keeping her most intimate thoughts to herself, she had created her own legend, the existence of which delighted her.

Beside her sat Julie Angeot, better known as Lily, a girl who had little more to offer by way of seduction than the youthfulness of her eighteen years. Where had Berthe found her? They'd arrived together for an evening of smoking one night at Courvoisier's, and Berthe had treated her to twelve pipes of opium. The girl thought she was going to die. Courvoisier couldn't recall without laughing how, while she was vomiting into his sink, Berthe had held her head and repeated:

"Puke it up, my dear; puke it up, my little girl; you're losing your virginity."

Everyone, even Auportain, had gone through this terrible ordeal their first time—the painful bouts of nausea, the retching, the cramps in the abdomen. A veritable bout of seasickness that strips the neophyte smoker of all dignity, all willpower, all strength. They were able to smile while watching the others go through it, but in their memory they still preserved the image of their own first night, and of the final degradation that had heralded their initiation.

For Antoine Maison, this had happened at Barbara's the year before, on 14 July. It was through her that he'd first encountered the drug, and it was through the drug that he was trying to get to know her better. He had vivid memories of the trip back home when, around four in the morning, beneath a whitening sky, she'd taken him, lifeless, in her big open touring car back to his apartment in Montmartre, through the outdoor parties that had opened to let them pass before closing in their wake.

Back in the present, Antoine was pleasurably sinking into a swamp of dreams and optimism. Reverie was taking hold of him. He stopped smoking, lit a cigarette, drank some lemonade, and settled himself into the cushions. The opium's fragrance stirred his thoughts. His future—already, it seemed, a part of the past—was filled with hope. Images of the things he wanted washed over him like a tide, rushing through his head with a stunning swiftness. He overcame any and all obstacles, undertaking wild adventures as his surroundings faded away. It seemed as if hours had gone by. He looked at his watch. It'd barely been fifteen minutes since he'd entered his dream world. Beside him, Auportain was smoking methodically. A deep inhalation brought the smoke into his lungs as he tilted the bowl over the flame. Then, slowly, he released it in thick coils. Antoine sank back into the darkness. When he again became conscious of his surroundings, everyone was isolated in their own personal universe. Barbara was the only one still smoking. Antoine got up and went to lie down beside her.

"A pipe?"

"With pleasure."

She prepared it herself and handed it over to him.

"It's so nice here," she said. "In the summer, we'll be able to open the windows and the smell of flowers will mix with the opium. You feel so free then. No need to hide yourself away."

"I imagine that smoking at sea wouldn't be without its charms."

"Oh! I went up the Missouri on a yacht with one of my friends. It was delightful. But, listen, Antoine, do you think you're addicted?"

"Me? No . . . or at least I don't think I am."

"Did you smoke yesterday?"

"No, and not even the day before that . . ."

"Then you're not addicted. But it will happen to you just like it did to the others. It's not a great situation to find yourself in, you know. Keep your freedom as long as you can, things are much better that way. Although I do have a friend who never lets opium get the better of him. He starts using, spends six months puffing like a train, then gives it up from one day to the next without the slightest bit of difficulty. But he's the only person I know who can manage that."

Antoine was inhaling on the new pipe. Barbara guided the bowl toward the flame and, from the tip of the needle, simultaneously scraped away the blisters of dross.

"Do you like where you live?"

"Oh, it's just a basic hotel room in Montmartre."

"But it must be such fun! Can you see a panorama of Paris from your window?"

"No, just a dull, depressing street and an unimpressive view of the Sacré-Coeur between a couple of roofs."

"Oh, you ought to move . . . in Paris you can find marvelous apartments for next to nothing . . . You just need to put in a little bit of money and you've got yourself a palace . . ."

Antoine was thinking about the five hundred francs he spent each month on his lodging. The life that he'd dreamed of as an adolescent was already proving to be a farce. His hotel room symbolized an arduously won freedom over prejudices of caste, familial obstacles, and the struggle to earn a living. It now seemed to him, however, the very image of the mediocrity he'd been determined to escape. And opium gave him the illusion of already having done so. With the drug he found himself entering his chateau in la Belle du

Bois, a chateau in which, according to his mood, he could indulge his taste for solitude or host parties for his friends, who would all be charming, loyal, intelligent . . .

"Are you nodding?" asked Barbara.

"Yes . . . I was dreaming . . . I was dreaming about you."

"And of yourself as well. It's always like that . . . But what do you do in life? Since we've known each other, I've never heard you talk about yourself . . . I bet you'd like to make a tour of the world . . ."

"Oh, I'd love to, but it's not what I want most."

"And what would that be? Come on now, what do you want more than anything else in the world?"

"To find a hidden treasure . . ."

"How exciting that would be! Deep in some forest, in the ruins of a castle or an abbey . . . you dig . . . you dig . . . and find a chest filled with jewels that are three thousand years old, diamonds, turquoise, rubies . . . the scepter of Philippe the Fair, daggers made of ivory and gold, rings, and talismans just like the ones in novels about knighthood."

"I wouldn't ask for so much . . . no, just to find, in the corner of a meadow shaded by poplar trees, underneath several centimeters of dirt, a little pitcher filled with long-forgotten pendants decorated with effigies. And nearby there are three big mushrooms. A toad and grasshoppers jump through the grass, crickets go about their business, butterflies and birds fly around. There's the distant whistle of a train. On the horizon, a shepherd watches over his sheep on a hillside, and behind a hedge there's the sound of a hare running by. The air vibrates, the sun's hot, and a big white cloud speeds by in the sky, casting a soft shadow."

Barbara had set down the pipe and moved the tray to the side.

"Yes . . . and there would be two rings with signets engraved in emerald. And we'd each take one."

She put her hand on his shoulder and gave him a long kiss on the mouth. He embraced her with both arms and they rested a long time intertwined, head against head, chest against chest.

Suddenly, she freed herself from the embrace, lit a cigarette, and offered him the pack.

"They're Westminster's Commander . . . it's not easy to find them in Paris . . . unless you prefer Bocks, from Havana."

He placed his hand on her wrist.

"Barbara, don't you love me, at least a little?"

"Love? What do you mean? Yes, I love you just fine. But for love, real love, go ahead and do your best to find it. As for myself, I don't believe in it, or rather I don't believe in it anymore. Let's talk about something else . . . this will only ruin the night."

Antoine didn't know what to say. He resorted to her friends.

"Who's Arichetti?"

"Oh, he's delightful! The human embodiment of imagination. And so funny! He's another one of my little discoveries. I met him in Juan-le-Pins, or wait . . . no, in La Napoule. On a very hot summer day . . . I was sunbathing on the beach between La Bocca and La Napoule, when all of a sudden I saw a man, completely dressed, come out of the water: white shoes, white pants, blue shirt, and a blue and red tie. I thought I was dreaming. Finally, I said to him: 'Have you just come from Africa?' 'No,' he said, 'I walked here from Cannes. It was so nice out . . . but so hot, and the water felt so good! So I decided to walk through it.' At which point he undressed down to his underpants and set his clothes aside to dry. But the best part of it all was when he ironed them out with a rock heated by the sun! We left the beach together and went to eat, and then I took him to smoke several pipes. He was already in the habit."

"What does he do?"

"He's a correspondent for some big American firm whose details I've forgotten. Or rather he was. I think he had problems with them, so they gave him a big compensation package to get rid of him. That's how he was able to buy that beautiful car of his."

"Does he still have money?"

"No. But he'll always be able to make it. He's extraordinarily talented. If he wanted to start working as an interior decorator, he would make a fortune. Paris's upper rungs are crazy about him . . . Another pipe?"

"I'm going home . . . Arichetti will take us back . . ."

This came from Columot, who was standing nearby with Marie-Jacqueline.

"Home? what time is it?"

"It's five, my lovely Barbara."

"Already!"

Arichetti, Columot, Marie-Jacqueline, and Lily left together, the sound of the powerful automobile resounding for a long time through the night air. When it was quiet again, Antoine entered a long tunnel of golden thoughts, which he abruptly came out of to discover that it was day. Barbara and Berthe were lying on a divan, wrapped in bathrobes and blankets. Courvoisier was lighting a cigarette in front of the door to the garden. Auportain was holding his hat.

"My dear sir, would you care to join me? We'll go for a walk along the Marne or in the Bois de Vincennes. Barbara and Berthe are staying for a while longer, that is, until five in the evening, and we can let Courvoisier speed home in his car."

Antoine stood up. He drank down a large glass of orangeade, washed his face, and went out with his companion. A faint mist hung over the Marne. Their surroundings seemed to be an extension of the night's ambiance. They went along wordlessly, with the sensation of floating through a cloud. The sound of a motor approached; then came the voice of Courvoisier:

"Doctor, it's a very bad idea to walk in the fog. Climb in. I'll drop you off wherever you want . . . Weren't you saying something about the Bois de Vincennes?"

And so the three of them took off together, Antoine relieved to have not left Courvoisier behind but still uneasy about the idea of Barbara staying at Artenac's.

Several minutes later, Courvoisier let them off on a path in the Bois de Vincennes. Then he started off again, almost hitting a lone cyclist, and disappeared around a bend.

"Where is he off to so fast?"

"Nowhere important, my dear Antoine. He got up this morning with a big plan in mind. No doubt he's driving to his laboratory to work. But will he make it that far . . . or will he lose his enthusiasm before he does? I watched him last night while you were lost in your dream of Barbara. He was alone on a divan, a lamp lighting up that attractive face of his. Suddenly he wanted to jot something down and took out his pen. A wasted effort, however, since he put it back in his pocket without having written a word. He left in search of his dream. Should we hope he finds it? I'm not so sure. Likely his inspiration, whatever idea might have entered his head, will prove to be mediocre."

The path had led them to an expansive lawn. A gardener was cutting the grass. A light breeze carried along several stray blades. They sat down on a bench. Auportain had fallen quiet, and Antoine, somewhat disoriented, had no desire to break the silence. He was enjoying the beautiful morning. He felt as if he was being lifted up by invisible wings. The ambient fragrance seemed to penetrate the entirety of his body. He was conscious of his breathing, and of the great pleasure he felt in taking the fresh air into the deepest recesses of his body, his heart, his spirit.

Barbara lived in a large apartment in Auteuil, though most of the rooms went unused. The living room served as a studio, and she hardly went anywhere else besides the bathroom. The windows opened onto a panorama of houses, out of whose disorder the Eiffel Tower shot up. Further on could be seen the line of hills in the inner suburbs, which were covered with thick forest. In the clearings, one could make out the buildings whose light pierced the thickness of the night.

When Antoine arrived, Barbara was alone. She lived without servants so as to have more freedom, limiting herself to a single cleaning woman who came by for several hours in the morning. She was wearing a white housecoat and, after letting the young man in, she went back to sit in an armchair situated in front of an open window. A bottle of brandy was set on the ground, and a half-full glass dispersed the light shining through it out over the gray carpet. Antoine suddenly found himself overcome by a feeling of faintness. It was as if his skull had been entirely emptied of cerebral matter and all that remained was an immense hollowness that made his head spin. He didn't know what to say, was unable to think of a single sentence worthy of articulation. The moment he'd been anticipating for weeks now was turning into a torment. For several days he'd thought of nothing but seeing Barbara, feeling something similar to the joy he'd experienced, as a younger man, when the time came for this party, that outing, this vacation. And now, had it been possible, he would have run away. He considered making an excuse for an early departure but couldn't even summon the energy to do that. He drank his brandy while looking over Barbara, whose face, with its closed eyes framed by thick blonde curls, had taken on an expression of deep tranquility. Her neck was solidly attached to her muscular shoulders, and beneath her outfit's light fabric he could make out the contour of her breasts, her stomach, her hips. Through the slit of her dress, her legs, at once fragile and firm, were exposed up to the middle of the thigh. A mule swayed at the end of her foot. But what really gave her body its voluptuous appearance was neither the beauty of her limbs, stomach, or chest, nor the youthful radiance of her complexion, nor the vulnerability expressed in her posture. It was the calm intake of air that caused her chest to rise and, between her gleaming teeth and through her slightly open, half-smiling mouth, seemed almost visible. The various sounds of the world were muffled by the walls, and the room seemed to be filled with little more than this steady breathing, which had imposed its own rhythm onto the passage of time. Antoine felt as if he'd matched his own breathing with Barbara's and that, by doing so, he'd penetrated the world of her daydream.

"Barbara," he said.

She didn't respond. She was asleep. Antoine was grateful for this, since it saved him from a conversation during the course of which he knew he'd embarrass himself. He was careful not to make even the slightest sound. He filled his glass carefully and, holding it in his hand, entered a labyrinth of imagination. The present moment had taken on the immobility of a vast and empty space, and he found himself comfortably suspended between desire and reality. Sometimes a tugboat's horn, a bird's song, a whistling train, or the hum of a car would pass between them. A sigh would make her throat swell, and then she'd return to her private domain. Drawn-out minutes went by. The doorbell suddenly broke the mood. Barbara awoke with a smile and stood up. He glimpsed her two slender thighs. She ran a hand over her hair as she passed by him.

"I think we fell asleep," she said.

She opened the door. Lily's voice could be heard, then kisses and a series of words . . . darling . . . tea . . . sleeping . . . They came together into the room.

"So, Antoine, basking in the sun, are we?"

Space was contracting. Soon, the smoking lamp would be lit on the divan, tea would be steaming in their glasses, and the usual ceremony would start once again. Antoine reproached himself for his cowardice. He should have spoken while he'd had the opportunity. How many months would it be before he found himself in that same situation, with that precious one-on-one privacy? Inside himself, he felt a hatred flare up against Lily for disturbing them.

"Antoine is so silly," she said.

"It's your fault, Lily . . . You woke him up! The two of us were perfectly content to be sleeping, with the fresh air drifting in. If you hadn't arrived, we would have been in the same place until morning."

"Don't try to put all the blame on me. You would have eventually needed some bamboo."

The three of them stretched out around the tray.

"Barbara," said Antoine, "I took your advice. I found a charming place between the boulevard and Montmartre. A quiet street. A big old building with gardens just outside the windows. I think

Chopin and Musset used to live there. Or at least that's what they told me . . ."

"Oh! Will you have me over?"

"You'll be the first to see it, Barbara, when everything's set up. I think you'll like it."

"What about me? I don't get to come and see it?"

"Of course you do, Lily. You'll come and so will the rest of our friends. There's a big moss-covered fountain in the garden, and giant trees filled with birds. It feels like you're far away from Paris . . ."

In the evening, Barbara asked Antoine to go look for a pack of cigarettes in the bathroom. Wet towels were scattered on the floor, alongside stockings and shoes. Disorganized bottles of makeup and perfume sat on the dressing table. A half-closed faucet dripped water into the sink.

He found the cigarettes on a glass shelf. He grabbed them but, just as he was going out, he paused a moment to stare at an open box of suppositories sitting beside a lighter.

Artenac was packing. Flannels and woolens, festive ties, and various other articles of clothing were piled on his bed. The young man went about his task leisurely. Soon, everything had been packed into two light brown leather bags. The only thing left to deal with was a half-open case, which contained a pair of pajamas, a bottle of cologne, several boxes, a kit. Already dressed for his trip, Artenac checked the time. Eleven in the morning, and the train wasn't leaving until eight o'clock at night. From a drawer, he took out a white paper package. "Twenty grams of heroin here and twenty grams in the bag. That's more than enough to get myself clean in three months. But how am I going to measure out a gram with no scale?" He then remembered a method that Courvoisier had described to him.

He spread out the dull, white powder onto a cross-ruled sheet of paper. With the help of a ruler he shaped it into a rectangle ten centimeters in length. He leveled it out and, using a penknife, separated a five-millimeter-wide line and put it into a phial. Then he boiled some water, let it cool, and poured in the powder. He inserted the emery stopper, put it all into the case, took it back out, and then placed it inside his pocket alongside a flat box that contained a syringe. Satisfied with his work, he went to have lunch at Mother Lampion's.

"Ah, there you are! I hope you've got an appetite. I have pike fillets with white butter sauce and guinea fowl . . . It's delicious.

"Perfect. Treat me well, seeing as how this will be the last time you'll see me before winter."

"Is that so? Are you taking off for the countryside?"

"I'm going to spend three or four months on the Côte d'Azur."

"Wonderful . . . I hope that'll do you some good. You've looked pretty lousy these past few weeks. Take care of yourself and come back hungry. Are you leaving today?"

"Eight in the evening."

"Good, then you have time for a proper meal. You won't be eating this well in the Midi . . ."

Around three o'clock, to kill time, Artenac set off in a taxi for Paris. "I'll get my ticket and come back for my bags around six."

At four, he stopped by at Berthe's. Having woken up late, she'd just come out of the bath and her unmade-up face sprung out freshly from her terry cloth bathrobe.

"Artenac . . . what a great idea! I was just about to have my tea . . . and my breakfast . . ."

She unhesitatingly brought out the opium tray along with another one carrying the tea.

"So, what's new with you?"

"I'm leaving for Marseille this evening."

"Marseille? Are you going to restock straight from the source?"

"No, I've decided to slow down a bit, and where better to do it than where there's sunshine? I'm not taking anything besides my supply of heroin."

"Ah . . . You've decided to start snorting?"

"No, injecting. It's safer. It's also more efficient, and much more practical."

"Safer? I'd be careful if I were you."

"Oh, I've looked into it. You need less of the drug and it's not something you can do out in the middle of the street."

"Well, you'll surely smoke two or three pipes before leaving."

And so they smoked. At about five thirty, Jeanne Marjolain showed up and stretched out alongside them. Come seven, he was still smoking. He decided to put off his departure until the next day, and they had a meal consisting of tea, toast, jam, and fruit.

"I'll be in the sunshine down there, real sunshine, and I can spend my days in the water. I'm considering either Porquerolles or Port-Cros. I know a little place where I can go about things as I see fit. You have to slow down from time to time if you want to experience the full effect of the drug again. I'll come back ready for the winter, in top form and as black as ebony."

He'd put on his pajamas, and a rolled back sleeve revealed a skinny but well-toned arm.

At that very moment, his train was heading for Laroche.

He'd set his phial and syringe on a table. Berthe and Jeanne, despite themselves, were imagining the pleasures they could give and waiting for Artenac to offer them an injection. He was also in the mood for one.

Around midnight, he succumbed to temptation and went into the bathroom. He came back out and shut himself away inside a personal reverie, where the conversation between the two women reached him as nothing more than a distant hum. Disappointed and impatient, Berthe and Jeanne left him alone.

"It's delightful," he suddenly said to them, "and so much stronger. If you don't mind, I'll go into the bedroom now. I'll give you both an injection in an hour."

And he staggered out of the room.

An hour passed, and then another. Berthe decided to go check on him. When she came back out her voice was filled with anguish.

"Jeanne! Come quick, I'm worried. He's not moving or responding, and his forehead's gone completely cold."

Jeanne carried in a lamp and shined it over Artenac's face. It had turned yellow and beads of sweat had formed on it.

"He doesn't seem well."

"Oh God, what if something happens to him here? What should we do?"

"Ask Auportain to come over."

Berthe went straight to the phone. The doctor took a long time to respond, but at last he answered.

"What is it?"

"Doctor, did I wake you?"

"Yes."

"Doctor, can you come over, it's Berthe … Berthe Cassotte. Artenac's very ill."

To her great surprise, Auportain didn't make her plead with him.

"Fine, I'll come … while you're waiting, put hot bricks around his feet … keep him warm."

And then he hung up.

The two women attended to the sick man, covering him with blankets and coats … Not long after, Auportain arrived. He went straight to Artenac, took his wrist, carefully examined his pupils.

"Why did you wait so long to call me? He hasn't got a chance now. What the hell have you gotten yourselves into?"

From the mantelpiece, he took the syringe and the little flask.

"Morphine? Heroin?"

"Heroin," answered Jeanne.

"Such foolishness ... in what quantity? How strong is this solution?"

"I don't know. He brought it with him. He said he was taking it with him on a trip as a replacement for opium; that it took up less space and had a stronger effect."

"Indeed. I'm going to give him a shot of camphorated oil as a matter of form, but he's already a corpse."

He looked through his case, removed two phials, bent over Artenac . . . straightened up, took another glance at him.

"In five minutes he'll be dead, there's nothing to be done for him."

And he went into the neighboring room.

"So, what are you going to do now?"

"Can't we take him to a hospital?"

"Hospitals don't treat the dead."

"Then what do you suggest we do?"

"I don't suggest anything. I've already told you not to rely on me in these kinds of situations. I'm a selfish old man. With the help of opium, I've found a pleasant way to live out the last part of my life. I have no children, no wife, no body of work to complete. I've been happy to lay my old sorrows to rest. But at your age, you'd have to be a pair of idiots without any hope of recovery to waste your beauty, your health, hell, your entire life with this trash. A lot of good it's done you! Anyway, I can't do anything . . . but I do hope this serves as a lesson for you."

And with that he left.

Neither Berthe nor Jeanne moved. Eventually, Berthe went to check on Artenac. His glazed-over eyes seemed to be staring directly at her. She took him by the hand. It was cold, and sticky with sweat. She shut off the lights and went back to Jeanne, who was gathering cigarette butts from an ashtray . . .

"Oh! Jeanne . . ."

"I think the doctor has a point, don't you?"

"What if we asked Courvoisier?"

"You do it, he doesn't like me as much as he likes you."

Before picking up the phone, Berthe took a bottle of perfume from the dressing table and poured it over her hand.

"Jeanne, if only you knew, it's dreadful . . . I touched his hand . . . ah, it's horrible . . .

And she began to turn the dial.

Courvoisier had eaten with Antoine then taken him home. In an ardent desire to entertain his companion, he'd rediscovered his charm. Antoine had questioned him at length about his work, and while explaining to him in simple language the nature of his research—using an account of the evolution of physics since the end of the eighteenth century as a prelude to the problem he was currently occupied with: the origin of cosmic rays—Courvoisier had felt a surge of enthusiasm.

"And when I say cosmic, my dear Antoine, that's only to use the same word that everyone else uses. Because, although we do know what they're made of, we don't know where they come from. Even the word ray is inappropriate. It's a phenomenon, the most important phenomenon of our time. But this thing that's imperceptible to our senses, this enormous force—and you'd need quite a set of armor to stop these . . . these projectiles—could revolutionize physics, and all our ideas concerning the universe. Or it could change nothing at all. You see, it always comes back to metaphysics. Every scientific discovery is a plot won in this imaginary forest. But anyone can be a metaphysician. Yourself, the village idiot, the greatest of geniuses. The physicist arrives. He weighs a cubic meter of air, or does whatever else it might be, and a whole heap of great metaphysical contraptions collapses and start rusting somewhere, in the great shed of hypotheses. It's nice to talk to you, Antoine. You seem interested in what I have to say. It's encouraging. I have a lot of notes that are all ready to be put into a book. I've been neglecting them. I had the feeling that I was working inside a vacuum. I think it's time to get back to work."

He was already taking out his smoking materials.

"How about a couple of pipes? We can keep on talking . . ."

And so began the night's procession. The drugs and the conversation intoxicated Courvoisier. Antoine, an immobile voyager, let himself be carried off into spaces whose immensity soothed him, leaving him breathless and at the same time imparting trust and courage. But he was both too experienced and too lucid not to foresee the disillusionment that would accompany the morning. The conversation had become sentimental. Courvoisier was now talking about friendship, which he was offering to his companion. Some indistinct and emotional sensation was both inside them and around them. Antoine would have liked to hold the other against his chest. But timidity prevented him from doing so, as well as the memory of the kiss from Barbara at Artenac's, the embrace which had convinced him that he'd won her over and from which she'd freed herself as nonchalantly as someone stepping out of a bath.

Suddenly the phone rang. Courvoisier answered it: "Yes . . . no? . . . what? . . . Auportain? Okay, I'm coming, yes, I'll come with Maison. We'll be there as soon as we can . . ." Then to Antoine:

"We have to go . . . something's happened to Artenac over at Berthe's."

Berthe, Jeanne, Courvoisier, and Antoine sat together in the dimly lit room. In a shadowy corner, the oil lamp gave off a pale and hazy light. The door to the bedroom where Artenac was laid out had been left open. Antoine might even have said that it'd been left wide open and, while the other three talked things over, he amused himself by comparing the two terms.

As soon as he'd arrived, Courvoisier had taken Berthe into his arms.

"My poor Berthe!"

"Raoul, Raoul, it's just dreadful what's happened. Help me, please."

They'd gone together toward the divan. Courvoisier got to work. Artenac was no longer moving; his eyelids didn't respond to light; his breath barely clouded a mirror; his feet and his hands were cold and moist with sweat.

And now the four of them sat together, without knowing what to do. Berthe was pitiful. She'd lost all her arrogance and all her vivaciousness. Everyone was sketching out desultory plans. Suddenly the doorbell rang. They looked at each other, terrified. It rang a second time, a third, and then came an impatient knock. Berthe got up to answer, but, first, closed the bedroom door, extinguished the oil lamp, and covered the tray with a blanket. Finally, she went to the entryway and opened the door. They heard her voice:

"You came back!"

Auportain entered with a case and a package. He passed wordlessly through the studio, opened the bedroom door, and turned on the light. Antoine and Courvoisier went in to join him.

"Make sure Berthe and Jeanne stay to the side. And you two, help me. Drive a nail into the top of the divan."

Meanwhile, he'd opened the package and taken out a large phial of serum. He was now unbuttoning Artenac's pants to expose his stomach. There was neither hammer nor nail in the apartment. The doctor handed the phial to Antoine, recommending that he hold it at a distance, then, with a long needle, he made an injection. For several minutes, they remained motionless and silent. Then . . .

"There's nothing to be done. His circulation's stopped."

He withdrew the needle, gathered up his materials, held out his hands to Raoul and Antoine.

"Farewell. I haven't seen anything. I don't know anything. There's nothing more that I or anyone else can do."

He went back through the studio, shrugging his shoulders. Berthe got up. She was about to speak, but decided against it. She turned on the stairwell light herself and softly closed the door, against which she then collapsed, sobbing. Courvoisier came up beside her and put his hands on her shoulders.

"There's no point in crying. Come on now. Everything's going to be fine."

She followed him back inside without taking the time to dry off her face. Next to the fireplace, Jeanne was looking at herself in the mirror and dabbing her eyes. That he was an attentive witness rather than an actor in a play seemed uncanny to Antoine, who still hadn't moved.

Because Artenac was no longer a consideration. His fate didn't worry his friends except regarding how it could lead them into a disaster. Saving him would have been best, of course, but was saving him the point? The goal was to save oneself, to save Berthe so as to save oneself. Courvoisier's nostrils were pinching. He spoke hesitantly. Soon, he gave in.

"I'm going to smoke a pipe. I can't stand it anymore. I haven't had my dose. Do you mind, Berthe?"

And right away he was relighting the pilot light, sticking a needle into the jar of opium. The drug was soon sizzling on the bowl.

"Ah, my God, save him!"

This was the wish repeated aloud by Berthe. A selfish wish, because in reality she'd already removed Artenac, as a living man, from the scope of her concerns. Antoine remembered that there was a crucifix hanging above the bed in which Artenac lay. Was this faith, when God was called upon only to prevent personal misfortune? As for himself, he preferred the primitive faith of the Tirailleurs in Morocco.

It had happened in Fez. He was being treated in a hospital, while also acting as secretary to the medical officer. One night they'd brought in a Senegalese Tirailleur. They put him to bed, and he slept until morning. When he awoke, he was showing all the symptoms of malaria. Antoine himself drew the blood, through several needle insertions into a fingertip, and spread it out onto a group of glass slides. By the afternoon, the Negro had stopped moving. Toward evening, he started scratching at his sheets then, tossing and turning, threw off his covers, revealing a muscular stomach and a sexual organ that stood as straight as an exclamation mark. The nurse had Antoine called in to calm the patient. Then everyone had gone to sleep. Around midnight, the Arab watchman called on Antoine.

"You come. The Negro is no good."

And indeed he wasn't. He was standing up and threatening invisible demons with the entirety of his impressive musculature and clenched, outstretched fists. Antoine approached fearfully, but the Negro let himself be put to bed without resistance. Antoine tucked him in while someone else went to get the medical officer. Then the Negro buried his head into Antoine's chest. When the medical officer arrived, he was dead. It would be a long time before Antoine forgot that night. They'd piled up the Tirailleur's clothes and set everything, corpse and rags, onto a stretcher, which was subsequently taken to the hospital morgue. But, while picking up the chechia, Antoine had felt something beneath his fingers; it was a cracked lion's paw with hair stuck to its interior ... almost certainly the hair of a marabou. He took the gris-gris and put it into his pocket. Coming back from the morgue through the hospital gardens, he suddenly ran into four or five gigantic shadows: Senegalese Tirailleurs. They said that they'd come because their friend had just died. But how could they have known? He'd succumbed less than an hour before. And their camp was more than an hour's walk away! They asked to see his clothes, to take back his belongings. Antoine watched as they made an exhaustive search of the chechia, turning it every which way before reluctantly leaving. He'd kept the gris-gris right up until the day of his departure from Africa. Embarking from Casablanca, he still had it; debarking at Bordeaux, it was gone. He'd never come up with a good explanation for its disappearance . . .

Where was he? What did this vision mean? this memory?

He was at Barbara's, and Artenac was dead or dying, and he was hearing but not following Berthe and Jeanne's conversation, to which Courvoisier, between pipes, would make some small contribution.

Suddenly a moan came from the darkened bedroom.

"He's alive!" Berthe cried out, as she dashed in his direction.

Courvoisier completed an inhalation and then followed her. Antoine also went shortly after. But Artenac was still motionless.

"He can't die here!" screamed Berthe. "He can't!"

Antoine came of out his reverie.

"Who says he's going to die? Auportain's not the only doctor in Paris. Let's call someone else."

"No! No! I don't trust anyone else. If Auportain says he's going to die then he's going to die."

"Hey," said Courvoisier, "what if we take him back to his house?"

"And then what?"

"If he's already gone, what does it matter? They'll think he's traveling, and the body won't be found for weeks. We can take him in my car. No one will notice us at this hour."

"I'm not going, I don't have the stomach for it!"

"Neither do I," added Jeanne.

"Fine, Antoine will help me."

Antoine would be unable to think back on the descent in the elevator, when all this was over, without a pang of disgust. With great difficulty, they'd redressed Artenac, and the struggle Antoine had gone through to put his shoes back on would stay with him for a long time. And then, in the elevator, the two of them had had to hold him up, slack, inert, already a corpse.

Berthe and Jeanne met them in the lobby.

"We don't want to be alone after all that. We'll come with you."

They went through the lobby without making a sound, the click of the door the only noise that broke the silence. Then, in the darkness, headlights off, they put their dying friend into the car before all getting in themselves. But then Courvoisier realized that he was almost out of gas. Could they risk going to a garage?

Two policemen arrived. Courvoisier told them that he was having car troubles.

"There's a gas station two hundred meters from here, but it doesn't open for another hour. The best thing to do is stay put and then go get a canister."

And with that, they left.

The wait, in the motionless automobile, seemed interminable. They lit cigarette after cigarette and spoke, in between long periods of silence, in subdued voices. A state of torpidity was coming over them. They could hear the sound of powerful trucks and the steady beating of hooves from horse-led trash carriages coming from somewhere near the boulevard de Courcelles. The four still living individuals shut themselves away in their dreams, their memories, their hebetude. The excitement had delayed the drug's effect. It was again exercising its sentimental and stimulating effects. In the front, Berthe and Jeanne tightened themselves against Courvoisier, who was mechanically waiting, as his imagination went on whirring, for the first rays of light and the sound of clocks.

In the back, Antoine was alone with the cadaver. It seemed to him as if deathly odors were already being given off by the body that, just several hours earlier, had been a lively young man, animated by a life-sustaining flow of blood.

"When I think," said Jeanne, "that if he'd taken his train . . . by now he'd be speeding through the Rhone Valley, somewhere between Valence and Avignon."

"Poor guy! He'll never get a chance to see the Mediterranean again."

At last, Courvoisier opened the door.

"It should be open now."

He seemed to be gone for a long time. Finally, he came back with two canisters and emptied them into the tank.

"There we go! Now we're set for a hundred kilometers."

He started the engine and took off. At boulevard de Courcelles, he turned left and came to place Clichy.

"Where are you going? You should have headed straight for the Seine along boulevard Malesherbes, la Madeleine, and la Concorde."

"You're right. I guess I was distracted. Damn . . . via Gare Saint-Lazare . . ."

But he'd already gone past the square and didn't want to turn around. Via place Blanche, he came to rue Notre-Dame-de-Lorette, then Montmartre.

Courvoisier drove recklessly. The streets, at first empty in the western neighborhoods, soon came to life. It didn't occur to Courvoisier to avoid Les Halles, and they soon found themselves in the middle of a throng of porters, merchants, other cars. Sunlight shone on the piles of carrots and turnips, cabbages and tomatoes. Seasonal flowers went by in the arms of buyers while the murmur of the morning crowd was like a song of springtime. Antoine held up Artenac, whose head was now tossing loosely about. His closed eyes, his waxy complexion, his pinched nostrils—all of it indicated the arrival of death. Sometimes the car came to a sudden stop, and the lifeless body would jerk forward. When it started off again, it fell back into Antoine's arms; he worried constantly that one of the very near passersby would catch sight of the cadaver. But the people outside, cheerful and talkative workers, saw no further than Jeanne and Berthe, seated next to Raoul. It was to them that they dedicated their gentlemanly compliments, all while wishing for every imaginable catastrophe to befall this nuisance of a car and its clumsy driver. At last they came out of the crowd and, via place du Châtelet, reached the embankment.

Only then did Courvoisier turn around.

"How's he doing?"

"Bad . . . very bad . . . I think he's dead."

"Dead?" said Jeanne. "Do you really think so?"

"You must be joking," Berthe added.

But the three of them looked back, and, seeing Artenac's face and Antoine's pale complexion, didn't say another word. Courvoisier sped up. He felt as if he were split in two, or rather turned inside out. He was acutely aware of both his physical movements and the changes in his mood, similar to times, long ago, when he was in his lab looking over physics experiments and equations.

Jeanne, her eyes staring straight ahead, was deep in her own thoughts. Her expression indicated that she was again feeling the effects of the drug. Opium was coming back to her brain in waves, which brought with them strange and distant memories. For instance, the day—she must have been about five years old, with her nanny—when a woman had said: "What a lovely child . . . she'll be quite the looker in another ten years." The memories were overpowering her. She had a burning desire to lie down and stay motionless and not feel the jolts of the car.

To not move, to be far away . . . such were the thoughts of Berthe as well, who, in some small corner of her brain, was singing incessantly to herself: "She had such tiny little feet, Valentine . . ." Why the hell was this song in her head? She remembered. Just several minutes before, in Les Halles, a deliveryman was whistling it as he pedaled along on his tricycle.

Antoine was beginning to feel nauseous. This whole affair seemed ridiculous. He was already imagining the embellishments Courvoisier, Berthe, and Jeanne would add to their retelling of it. But none of this mattered much to him. He watched the Seine, where the sunlight played with the shadows of the bridges and the iridescent reflections of oil. Tugboats, barges . . . and, here and there, a carefree idler watching the water and taking in the weather.

The car passed the Charenton postern.

"Lucky for us, they've done away with the octroi," said Jeanne.

Along a series of back roads, Courvoisier made his way to the road that led to Nogent. They passed the Rendez-Vous des Pêcheurs, so spruce in the morning light; then, taking a right, they came to the alley and stopped in front of the small house's wooden double doors. Courvoisier rushed to get them open before driving the car into the courtyard and closing them behind him. Then he looked for the key, fumbled with the lock, and, with Antoine's help, carried Artenac to the couch in the small living room. Artenac's eyes were open and watched them with a dismal and frozen expression. Courvoisier waved a hand in front of the pallid face.

"He's not reacting. I can't feel his breath, and he doesn't have a pulse. He's almost cold."

"What do we do?"

"I don't know."

"Let's put him in his bed."

"We'll have to undress him and I don't think I can do that."

"Then let's leave him on the couch."

"Someone will see him from the door."

"Then on the chair in the bedroom."

With some difficulty, they set him beside the fireplace. He slid down several times and they had to use cushions to secure him into place.

"Can we get going now?" said Berthe.

"Wait another moment."

Courvoisier searched the furniture and body. He found a small container of opium and the large packet of heroin. He took them. He also took every last piece of smoking paraphernalia: pipe, tray, needle, lamp. On a silver lighter, he spotted a streak of opium.

"We need to wash it."

"Give it to me . . . as a memento of Artenac."

And Jeanne slid it into her purse.

Courvoisier closed the bedroom door, was the last one to come out of the living room, which he locked, and then went to the car and stored away his booty.

"What about the keys?" asked Antoine. "You're going to bring them?"

He went around the house, entered through the kitchen, went back into the bedroom, and set the bundle of keys on the mantelpiece. Then, having put the kitchen key into the interior lock, he closed the door behind him. The others had already settled back into the car. He sat down at the steering wheel.

"There . . . I have everything that might hint at drugs."

"No," said Antoine, "and fortunately not. You left a phial of heroin and a syringe behind the clock. And, trust me, it's for the best. If they find him soon enough to realize how he died, it's better that they find drugs."

Berthe and Jeanne said nothing.

"You're right," said Courvoisier. "Now, listen carefully. We're going to stop by the Rendez-Vous des Pêcheurs . . ."

"You can't be serious!" cried Berthe.

"We have to. We came here after a long night to look for Artenac and didn't find him. So we decided to get breakfast while we were here. Repeat what I say and be absolutely sure not to add anything. The less you say the better."

"This is too much!" concluded Antoine.

They went out, closed the door to the little courtyard, and shortly after went into the café. Mother Lampion was at the counter and watched them come in without surprise.

"Ah, my little group of scoundrels, the beautiful weather has brought you back!"

"You haven't seen Artenac, have you?"

"He must be well on his way by now. He had lunch here yesterday and told me he was leaving for Cannes in the evening, and for quite a long time at that. Four or five months. It should do him good . . . you should have seen how he looked . . ."

"What do you mean yesterday? So soon? I didn't think he was leaving for another week."

"He told me yesterday evening. Did you go to his house?"

"Just did. It's locked and no one's answering."

"Well then, he must be gone. But you shouldn't let that stop you from having your breakfast . . ."

"Of course not."

"And, seeing as how you're already here, an aperitif and lunch. I have some stewed eel to die for, and, but don't tell anyone else, a hare pâté, that's right, hare . . ."

Barbara had brought Arichetti, Columot, Marie-Jacqueline, Noëlle, and Jeanne to a house she'd rented close to Paris, in the valley of the Yonne. Columot had driven them briskly there, but they'd still arrived after nightfall. For dinner, they prepared their own plates, and it was already late when they'd set up the divans and smoking material. This was when they realized that they didn't have any oil for the lamps. Barbara didn't want to ask for any from the neighbors, country folk she'd never met and didn't dare wake up. Columot proposed that they make do with heroin, but Barbara insisted on opium. Arichetti proposed to go look for some in the neighboring town. Noëlle found candles and tried to make use of them. The result was deplorable. The candle started smoking and the opium tasted like burnt fat. Arichetti left with Barbara, Marie-Jacqueline, Noëlle, and Jeanne in the car. Pont-sur-Yonne, Villeneuve-sur-Yonne, Saint-Julien du Sault all were sleeping. After Villevalliers, they knocked on the door of an inn. When the proprietor, who addressed them from an upstairs window, heard that they were looking for oil he simply closed the casements, saying that he didn't offer his services to drunkards. They continued their search. Joigny rested in thick darkness. At the hotel Ducs de Bourgogne, a drowsy maid told them that the kitchens were locked and that she couldn't wake either the chef or the owners. They were just about to set back off when their headlights fell upon two soldiers.

"Wait a moment, and let me try something," said Arichetti, who, in a low voice, went to ask the two men where he might find a brothel.

"There we are," he said as he got back in, "I know where we can find it, but it's not a proper place for the four of you. I'll go in alone."

"What are you talking about, Arichetti? I know how to handle myself anywhere."

"Of course, Barbara, it wouldn't be the most trying thing we've even been through . . ."

"Then tell us where you're going. Is your grocer a duke or a marquis?

"No . . . listen . . . I'm going to a house . . . well, a club . . . a brothel."

"Oh, a whorehouse! you should have said so. We'll all go together and have ourselves a good time . . ."

"Okay, but I've warned you . . ."

They went in, with Barbara leading the group, to a low-ceilinged room where three noncommissioned officers and two young customers were drinking white wine with four of the establishment's residents. A silence descended on their entry, and the owner herself came to take their order.

"You should know that I don't have the right to receive ladies. But these gentlemen will be discreet. I have champagne for a hundred francs per bottle."

"We'll take six of them," said Barbara. "These ladies and gentlemen will agree to keep us company."

Then, leaning over to Jeanne, who had the heroin, she whispered several words, took her purse, and left. When she came back, she had a small amount of white powder beneath her nostrils. She gave the purse back to Jeanne, who then left with Marie-Jacqueline. Almost immediately, Noëlle got up to join them. The four young women remained silent and listened to Arichetti recount his years of service to the three sergeants.

"Our major was a real madman. He had his horse arrested after it tossed him to the ground, and the punishment was read out at the company briefing. And you weren't allowed to laugh."

"I had one like that, too. He had his wife and children arrested. His orderly told us about it. He was extraordinary during the war. He would come out of the trench with his watch in his hand and scream out to the Germans: 'Germans! you have two minutes to shoot me down.' And the bullets would go roaring past him! But he wasn't even scratched!"

"Well, as for myself, I was thrown in both prison and the guardhouse. I did almost two months of extra service."

"It helps you come into yourself."

A woman had bent toward Barbara and begun speaking to her quietly:

"Say, could you give me a little?"

"A little what?"

"You know what I'm talking about. You left to have some earlier. There's still some under your nose."

Barbara took out her compact and looked at herself.

"Come on, give me some. I won't tell anyone."

"In a minute . . . I don't have it on me; wait until our friend comes back."

Because Arichetti had left the room to take his turn. When he came back his conversation partners were clumsily trying their hands at card tricks. He took the deck and amazed them. He imitated a magician's banter and looked them attentively in the eyes. Then suddenly he set down the pack and addressed the owner:

"Madame, would you be so kind as to sell me a small bottle of oil?"

"A bottle of oil? What kind of trick are you going to do with that?"

"It's not for a trick, it's for my salad … I eat one every night before going to bed … with lettuce … I can't sleep without it … and it so happens that I've run out of oil."

"And it really helps you fall asleep? I'll have to tell my husband. He can go entire nights without sleeping."

Shortly thereafter, she brought him a small phial. Arichetti then grew restless.

"It's getting late, we ought to be on our way."

"Hey, come on, aren't you going to give me a little?"

The girl had come up to Barbara and taken her by the arm. Barbara took the packet from Jeanne's purse and passed it to her under the table. Arichetti paid, stood up.

"Let's get going."

He went quickly out to the hallway that led to the exit. The others followed. He was almost running by the time he'd entered the impasse. He hurried everyone into the car and then started off abruptly, whispering to Barbara, who was seated beside him:

"It's the police. They're cops!"

His voice was so distressed that she didn't know how to respond. The headlights were dimmed, and Arichetti chose his route at random, making sharp turns. Two or three times Barbara thought he was going to go off the road, and, at one point, the fender scraped the parapet of a small bridge. The other three were asleep in the back. Suddenly a light reflected off the windshield, and Arichetti turned onto a dirt road and extinguished the lights. A powerful car passed by on the road, driving along at a fast and steady pace. Arichetti reversed, made a difficult U-turn, and took off through a maze of roads in which it was nearly impossible for him to find his way. They suddenly found themselves on a large street lined with workers' houses. They stopped in front of a building, behind which puffed a locomotive. Two trains went howling past each other.

"A station! But this is Laroche! Are you crazy? Where are you taking us?"

"We're saved! I've saved you, and myself as well. But we shouldn't lose any more time."

He oriented himself along the train tracks, started back toward Joigny, and then sped through the town. Several kilometers further on, he swerved. The car was now going over soft ground.

"Great! You've driven us straight into a field . . . come on, give me the wheel. I'll get us back, if the car's still running."

Barbara managed to find her way without too much difficulty while, at her side, Arichetti went on shaking, chattering his teeth, and repeating:

"My sweet Barbara . . . the police . . . they understood everything. The card trick thing, that's a classic. They pretend to take a card from your pocket or your purse, and then they check to see if you have any drugs. That's why I wouldn't let them do it. Fortunately, very fortunately, I know how to handle these kinds of situations. That stunt I pulled for the oil showed you how crafty I can be. They didn't understand a thing! But, still, they had a hunch. They're after us . . . drive fast . . . faster, for the love of God . . . or we'll all be in prison before noon."

Barbara stopped the car, lit a cigarette, and said, calmly:

"Arichetti, you're driving me crazy. Don't say another word or I'll drop you off on the side of the road and you can take care of yourself. There's not the slightest sign of the police anywhere. Besides, we weren't exactly shrewd, were we? They could see the heroin on our noses . . . Little Carmen asked me for some and I gave it to her."

"You gave it to her! Oh, we haven't got a chance now. Let's just hope they didn't get the car's number."

"Be quiet."

He obeyed, but when, around dawn, they reached Pont-sur-Yonne, he touched her shoulder.

"Let me out here. There's a train soon. I'm going back to Paris. I'd prefer that."

"If that's what you want . . . This never ends . . ."

He opened the door and got out before she'd had time to come to a full stop. The headlights flashed over him an instant, then Barbara took back off, shrugging her shoulders as she accelerated. In the middle of the countryside, she stopped again and turned around. Jeanne, Marie-Jacqueline, and Noëlle were sleeping together in a heap. The dreary tint of the car's interior light shone over their gaping mouths. Makeup had begun to come off under their eyes. Wrinkles could be seen. Barbara thought of the girls back at the brothel in Joigny. At this hour they must have been sleeping with the three subofficers or one of the civilians.

"What a mess!" she muttered.

She took Jeanne's purse, looked for the packet of heroin, snorted some, and started slowly back down the road in the cool morning air. The fields gave off a pleasant fragrance. There was light in the windows of certain farmhouses. In a yard she saw a muscular young man, or, rather, his silhouette. He swung a lantern as he headed for the stables, and several unleashed dogs followed behind, barking. In a village, a white cat was crossing the street. She slowed down so as to not hit it, turned off the headlights. It was day, and the house was close. In front of her, at a turn in the road, the flowers of a red chestnut tree were opening up behind the wall of a garden. A lingering owl went by, its flight as smooth as velvet, and took refuge in the shadows of a dilapidated house. She stopped again.

Clocks rung out across the countryside, harmonizing with each other from one village to the next, and even between the houses, in which the deep sound of pendulums brought to mind the smell of creamy milk, of coffee, of toast and butter. Long-forgotten Sundays came back to her. There were brioches, pale-colored dresses, the brightness of dreams, the world's extraordinary precision when seen through the eyes of a child. She pondered all this with her chin on the steering wheel. There was nothing to dread in that not-so-distant time. Everything was simple. Your little friends, boys and girls, were nice or mean, restive or docile. The sun was golden. Now she felt as if she lived inside a mosquito net or an aquarium. Everything was complicated by an absurd shadow, a shadow she'd felt hanging over her for days, even at high noon. She looked back again. Her group of girls was still asleep. What would be the point of waking them up to say that it was morning in the most pleasant of seasons, that life was wonderful and worth living, even barefoot and in rags? As for Barbara herself, on this very day, well before the sun had set, she would be back among the bats and the owls of her vice.

She started off again. The car went along slowly, very slowly. In the grass she could see the stirring of insects, count the peppermint plants, look over the pink-gilled mushrooms in a meadow. She shook off the oppressive sadness bearing down on her and accelerated. Arriving back at the house, she saw Columot. Dressed in flannel pants and a blue shirt, he was shooting his revolver at a tree. The dull sound of the shots seemed unable to pierce through the thickness of the morning air. Upon seeing the car, he did a little dance step and unloaded an entire clip into the air. The sound was reminiscent of torn silk, and Barbara suddenly envisioned a dancer's evening dress being brusquely stripped off by some mythological hero. Columot came straight up to the car door and opened it.

"What a lovely sight! They seem to be doing well … and Arichetti? Where's that idiot?"

He took Noëlle and Marie-Jacqueline by the arm, led them into the house, came back out.

"They won't be waking up anytime soon. I put them in the blue butterfly room, you know what I mean … On the bed. We'll get them undressed soon enough. As for the other one … I'm going to put her in the bedroom of the Inconnue de la Seine."

He took her in his arms, led her away, came back out.

"And now I'm going to put Barbara in the bedroom of the gilded clock, where we'll tell each other all about our sorrows …"

Barbara surrendered. He took her into his arms and carried her across the garden. She could see the dew that must have been wetting the bottom part of his pants and, through half-closed eyelids, watched the tree branches stream past above his head. He laid her out gently on the bed. She felt him untying her shoes, removing her stockings after having undone her garters, removing her jacket, removing her dress, and, when she felt his muscular arms wrap around her body, she set her head against his shoulder and fell asleep crying.

She awoke to the sun's heat pouring over the bed. Columot's voice resonated through the room, making her quiver. It wasn't that it was loud, but rather that its frequency harmonized with her life. She had the strange sensation of being penetrated and saturated by this masculine voice, of experiencing its essence with the entire surface of her body. In the presence of this strong man, Barbara felt in no way small; instead, and contrary to his size, it was as if he enveloped her to her exact measurements. She listened to him unthinkingly and effortlessly. She was the inspiration behind each of his words, her entire being contributed to his reactions, to his movements. The air in her lungs passed through his mouth, and certain of his sonorously pronounced syllables resonated in her chest.

Columot was giving instructions to an employee on the phone. It was an abstract monologue, completely outside her domain of understanding, in which figures followed unknown names, in which professional jargon morphed into an indecipherable tongue.

She hadn't opened her eyes, but she could feel the muscle fibers in her limbs automatically stretching themselves out. She felt as if she were the person performing Columot's movements—movements she hadn't yet seen—as if she, now equipped with attributes foreign to her gender, were he. The feeling was above all characterized by an immense physical desire, a craving for caresses and embraces. It was as if she were the interior being of the very man she desired, his feminine double, his ideal twin . . .

She finally opened her eyes during one of the silences that interrupted Columot's speech. She looked at him. He was seated by the table and watching her as he spoke. They stared at one another with the same expression. At that moment she became abruptly aware of her nakedness, of the sun's light and heat playing off her breast and thigh, of the deep shadow emphasizing the curvature of her waist and a nearly exposed hip, of an arm hanging down to the carpet.

Columot hung up the phone, stood, and took her into his arms. She felt herself dissolve in his embrace and waited, trembling, for his possession. Cradling her, Columot whispered words whose meaning was of little importance but whose sound merged with the fragrance of his skin, warmed by the sun like a plum. She felt his body stretch out next to hers, conform to her position, while his mouth kissed her throat and eyes. She could feel the slightest shudder of this neighboring body . . . But what was he doing? The space around her and between them expanded and began to howl like an abyss. Columot's head rolled onto her breasts and she, knowing it would be best if she pretended not to notice, realized that he was crying. The moment had passed. This beautiful morning was already taking on the dimness of twilight. An immense feeling of distress penetrated her. She placed her hand on the young man's hair.

"It's nothing, my dear, it's nothing."

But, his eyes already dry, Columot sat up and began speaking.

"It's nothing? Of course it is . . . it's our entire life. A moment ago I thought we'd be able to love each other, Barbara. But opium won't let us. How pathetic! It's responsible for whatever escape Arichetti was trying to make. And it's responsible for making you inaccessible to me. It's made me impotent."

"No, no, it's nothing."

"It is. Don't think that we'll have another moment like this. It's over. It's already too late. And don't think that either you or I will stop taking the drug. You'd laugh if I told you I was planning to, and with good reason. Is all this, in the end, because of our incapacity to love? and isn't it this incapacity that drives us to smoke and snort? What are we afraid of? ourselves? of others? . . . I don't know. But it's a mess, a goddamned mess, and we're nothing but wretched souls."

They stayed stretched out a moment, in silence. Barbara was the first to get up and leave the room. She came back with a glass of whiskey, which she handed to Columot. They sat down on the edge of the bed and, by turns, drank from the glass. When it was empty she laid her head on her friend's shoulder, and he took a long kiss from her plump lips. But they knew, both of them, that this kiss was only sanctioning the same sorrow, the same suffering, caused by the emptiness in their hearts, by the infirmity of their drug-addicted muscles and nerves, and by the very excess of sentimentality that had caused this emptiness and weakness.

A leaking pipe is by no means an extraordinary incident. The one that occurred at Barbara's, however, proved to have unexpected consequences. The tardily informed plumber said that no one would be able to come until the next morning. When someone finally did arrive, he had to ring a long time before Barbara, alone in the house, came to answer. She opened with tousled hair, her eyes glazed over with sleep and dreams, in a simple negligee. Her attractive neck rose up out of a bathrobe, over which she'd slipped a dressing gown. It didn't hang down low enough to conceal the legs of her pajamas or the silk mules covering her sockless feet.

Barbara's mornings, despite the drug use and her fatigue, were still the mornings of her springtime. Had she been nude, her skin would have given off luxury perfumes, and too many well-tailored dresses had covered her body for it not to have developed a figure worthy of the prestigious fashion designer who'd cut them. As for the numerous details which the knowledgeable man recognizes immediately—the well-cared for feet, the hands that bore no evidence of hard work, the clear, smooth skin, the breath that, if not entirely fresh, at least wasn't repellant, the regularly washed and groomed hair—and which allow him to categorize a woman into a specific milieu and to determine her age, without confusing premature signs of aging with illness, the wealth of the whore with that of the wealthy lady, the beauty of a healthy woman whatever her condition with the made-up complexion of a sickly one, the young worker saw these only as a unitary whole. He was, simultaneously, stunned and intimidated. He belonged, however, to that extraordinary class of Parisian workers who, through some protective instinct, know how to hide their emotions under a layer of either nonchalance, insolence, or boldness.

Barbara showed him to the bathroom and went to lie back down. Her jewelry was scattered on a shelf, but she didn't have it in her to be suspicious of a manual worker, and, indeed, would have been more suspicious of her own friends. The plumber got to work. The sound of his hammer resonated off the radiator and spread, at first, though the whole apartment, and then through the whole building. Barbara fell asleep to this carillon.

She woke up. She remained stretched out an instant with open eyes, then, suddenly, remembered that the plumber was there, got up, and rushed to the bathroom.

When she entered, the young man, with the help of a file, was about to snort a small pyramid of drugs in front of the mirror. Barbara had left an open packet of it above the sink. The apprentice winked before carefully directing the white powder toward his nose.

"You're going to kill yourself!" screamed Barbara.

The plumber put the heroin back in the bag and turned around to face her.

"Oh, come on! It's just cocaine! You're not the only one who uses it, you know."

"Cocaine! That's not cocaine! You don't know what you're talking about! Cocaine's shiny . . . that . . . that's dull!"

"Of course it is! there's plaster in it. Dealers can be real thieves sometimes."

"No . . . that's not cocaine . . . it's heroin. Do you understand? Heroin! And, besides, how do you know anything about cocaine?"

"I guess you think that kind of thing is only for the rich. Anyway, there's no need to hassle me . . . Yes, I was going to have some, but it's your fault . . . Shouldn't have this stuff lying around like that. What if I was with the police and decided to turn you in?"

"Turn me in if you want, young man. Do you think I give a damn? If I interrupted you, it's because you would have died if you've never taken that before, and for no other reason. Here, let me show you how to do it . . ."

And with the file she helped him inhale a thin pinch of the powder. Then she herself took a dosage, which was about three times stronger.

"That stuff tastes awful, you know! Cocaine's much more pleasant."

"Wait a moment and you'll see . . . If you're done with your work, come in here . . ."

The drug had soon taken an overpowering hold of the plumber. He invariably passed though the stages of exaltation, eloquence, and dream, which were rendered even more pleasant by Barbara's presence and her intoxicating scent.

He sipped a fruit juice, the taste of which reminded him too much of Diabolo to seem bland.

"The first time I took cocaine was on rue de Lappe. A friend of mine who hangs around Montmartre brought it. Then I took it again with another guy who got a job as a porter in a dance club, a real dance club. Afterward, we went to dance at the Coliséum. The girls there are so pretty. They're real girls, not prostitutes. We also went to Moulin de la Galette. Or to Nogent."

"Nogent? Do you know Mother Lampion?"

"You know her, too? Well! I've been there lots of times."

And he continued his story with descriptions of blissful Sundays spent on café dance floors, of fleeting romances during Paris's most pleasant time of year, when lilac gives way to lily of the valley.

"And do you like being a plumber?"

"I like it without liking it. But you've got to find something to do when you don't have it in yourself to be a pimp or a gangster."

For Barbara, the conversation had a sour quality to it, like an unripe sloe. She found in it the charm of a wholesome life, of simple pleasures, of a happiness that, however mediocre it may be, was free of worry. She had forgotten that the man she was speaking to was himself touched by the same demon as her, and that his reminiscences were already a farewell the moment she'd exposed him to the more dangerous, demanding muse. Come evening, she lit the small lamp and prepared the smoking materials. And so the plumber was introduced to opium. There was no longer any question of him leaving. He spent the night at Barbara's and she gave herself to him, simply, with neither high expectations nor curiosity. She experienced no lust, no appetite. The utter confusion of her heart and mind aroused this bodily abandonment, which she would come to consider as something meaningless due to the small amount of true pleasure she took from these frivolous encounters.

Dondlinger, such was his name, only left her embrace, as per the custom, to go vomit. In the early morning he found himself on rue de Dimanche, his head throbbing and vibrating, his stomach upset, his limbs stripped of all strength.

To have Barbara over to his place, Antoine had to buy opium. He confided in Columot, who smiled at his friend's request.

"Go find Mademoiselle Muche! The piano teacher. To be honest, it's been a long time since she's given any lessons. She's a batty old lady, sly as a fox . . ."

"And I'll need a pipe, too."

"For pipes, there's Molinier, rue de Vaugirard. You'll find everything you need there."

"Where does Mademoiselle Muche live?"

"Avenue de Breteuil. I'm surprised you don't know her. You've really never heard of Mademoiselle Muche? The old woman whose clothes are all ruched and flounced?"

Columot was in a good mood, and he used a little raspy voice to imitate Mademoiselle Muche.

"I'm just an old maid . . . Mademoiselle Muche, the piano teacher. I feel as if I've been alive for a hundred years. This dreadful year might see the death of me. I'm just an old maid . . . Mademoiselle Muche, the piano teacher. I love lace. Oh yes, I love lace. Lovely black lace more than anything else. I'm just an old, respectable maid. However, I must admit, I've stolen. I've stolen black lace, lovely black lace from the big shops. There's nothing I love more than black and that's why I get so happy when I see a first-class funeral go by.

"A first-class funeral is just beautiful, with its plumes and the undertaker's assistants all done-up around the hearse, and the horse, or rather the horses, because there are several of them, those lovely, lovely horses.

"But when I die, and it could happen this very year, I won't have a first-class funeral, but it's all the same to me because I wouldn't be able to see the black plumes, the beautiful hearse, and the lovely horses. Death must be a great comfort and I love the horses that rear up and whinny. . . .

"I'm just an old maid, Mademoiselle Muche, the piano teacher. Most of my students were young girls. But I barely have any students these days. People say I'm too old. But I would have loved to have had some boys as students. They would have learned how to play and, later, when they were men, with beautiful black beards, they would have come to see me on my saint's day.

"I did have one. He turned out poorly. It wasn't my fault. And he wasn't even handsome; I've always believed that it's the handsome boys who turn out bad; but he turned out bad, too.

"I remember, it was during the evening when he came ringing at my door; I hadn't seen him for years.

"'Mademoiselle Muche, could you lend me five francs? I was passing through the neighborhood and I don't have my wallet.'

"'But I can't lend you five francs, my dear, I don't have any money.'

"He left as suddenly as he'd appeared. Four days later I saw his name and picture in the newspapers. He'd killed some old woman.

"All the same, I would have loved to have some boys as students. I'm just an old maid, Mademoiselle Muche . . . the piano teacher. And all I have is the memory of that boy and my memories of funerals . . .

"Do you remember Victor Hugo's funeral? Oh, such a lovely funeral! I was twenty at the time. Oh, the things one does at that age . . . Me and my friend Céline, who got married to a tax inspector from Toulouse, we woke at two in the morning and went to the Champs-Élysées. Céline's mother came along with us. We took along some things to eat: sausage, a cold chicken, even a jar of jam. Oh, such a lovely funeral! I've never seen so many people. Oh, and just imagine that when it was over . . . how to explain it . . . you understand . . . we'd been standing for hours and hours. We came back at two in the afternoon. You men, it doesn't make any difference to you, you understand . . . what I mean to say is that you can relieve yourselves, whereas for us women . . . By the end we all had the most dreadful expressions on our faces. There were even some who . . . well . . . in the copses of the Champs-Élysées . . . and I saw lacework panties discarded, beautiful lace panties tossed into the gutter by women who couldn't hold it back. But the person who astonished me the most was Céline's mother.

"'Look at the birds, high up in that tree,' she told us.

"We looked up, but didn't see a thing.

"'They're there, they are, look higher!'

"We looked as hard as we could, but we still didn't see anything.

"Then all of a sudden, I heard the sound of a fountain. It was Céline's mother relieving herself, standing up, one foot on the sidewalk and the other on the road. Believe it or not, but I'd never seen such a thing. Oh, it surprised me, really surprised mc . . . She of course didn't have any pants on . . ."

Columot was laughing heartily, and the old maid materialized before Antoine. He could recall the funeral rites, which a whole nation had taken part in. The scene was edged with haze, like a panorama of a battle. At the close of the ceremony, the great man rested beneath three levels of cellars, the wind blew every which way withered everlastings, laurels, and soiled lace panties, a hundred thousand women with tortured bladders and distraught faces squatted throughout the city, and an old woman, firmly planted on her two poor legs, was trying to make two young women look for invisible birds whose song resembled the sound of a fountain . . .

Arichetti had stayed in bed for two days and two nights. He had nothing left, no opium, no dross, no heroin, no money: fifty or so francs at most. He desperately needed something, even laudanum if it came to that. But his mind had become unbalanced. Awake at eight o'clock in the morning, he decided to send despairing messages to each and every one of his friends. He didn't have the strength to use the telephone. And, besides, terror seized him as soon as he picked up the receiver. They were listening to him, he was sure of it. The waiter at the café, the woman at the post office—they were copying down everything he said. The prefecture's wiretapping equipment was working day and night for him and him alone. Consequently, he took various precautions to mask the meaning of whatever he said and began expressing himself with an indecipherable obscurity. He sat down at his table, pen in hand. At eleven o'clock he became abruptly conscious of his surroundings. He'd unthinkingly covered some ten or so pages in mysterious symbols: a succession of minuscule squares, circles, and stars filled up all available space. He numbly looked over the evidence of his mental state, stood up, grabbed his hat, and went out. The fresh air hit him straight in the face with a warm, fine rain and a light wind, the latter of which carried with it the season's first dead leaves.

He stood motionless on the edge of the sidewalk, mumbling to himself, while passersby turned to stare. Suddenly an image forced its way into his mind. At Artenac's, Berthe had told him, there was a phial of heroin and a syringe on the mantelpiece, behind the clock. He now had a precise goal in mind. His tears dried up as if some external power had taken control of his body. He made his way to Nogent like a sleepwalker and reached the house after having carefully avoided the Rendez-Vous des Pêcheurs. It was one in the afternoon and doors were shut against the bad weather. The wall surrounding Artenac's house wasn't particularly high; he scaled it and fell down onto the other side. He went around into the garden and looked over the building. The doors and windows were closed, but the kitchen door's transom was half-open. He took an iron chair from the garden and used it to peer inside. By slamming the door shut when he was last there, Courvoisier had loosened the key somewhat from its lock. Arichetti fished for it with his belt and a piece of wire, was able to bring it up and then enter the house. He was hit by a stale but powerful odor. A large quantity of flies was buzzing around. Fortunately, the shutters were closed and the room was plunged into an aquarium-like half-light, which was augmented by the mantelpiece mirror. Arichetti went toward it, making sure not to look at the armchair in which, he knew, Artenac's cadaver sat rotting. He grabbed the bottle and syringe but, reflected pond-like in the mirror, he caught sight of the corpse's horribly decomposed face.

He ran into the kitchen and, recklessly, sunk a solution-filled syringe into his thigh. Then he left everything in a mess on the white wooden table, shut the door behind him, and left.

The police picked him up the next night near the Saint-Antoine market. The once joyous participant in festive evenings, the outstanding friend who'd been so easygoing, so witty, was now little more than an anonymous piece of human jetsam. Of his past, of his name, of everything that had brought happiness into his life, he hadn't the slightest recollection. He was now an animal that required little more than his daily dose of narcotics. He made no secret of his need at the station, where the secretary wavered between sending him to a cell or to the infirmary. He had three fits within the space of two hours, and the officers thought he was going to die. They took him to the hospital, where an injection gave him the eloquence of a tormented litigant. With poetic sophistication, he accused the demons of the night and secret societies of torturing him. Then he fell back into a silence from which he would only come out, though at regular intervals, like a ski lift, to demand the shot that would temporarily free him from the mental desert in which he would now be living.

Committed and off drugs, he became the plaything of an administrative system that sent him, in a manner not unlike that of a damned soul descending through the circles of Hell, from various hospitals to various asylums, tormented all the while by the resounding clangs of heavy locks, illusory but unpickable, that dark powers shut endlessly behind him. Deceased—with a form in a filing cabinet as his only epitaph, which was itself destined to oblivion in some attic—but still living by means of the basic requirements for the continuation of elementary physical life, Marie-Louis Arichetti, twenty-seven years old, a victim of the discrepancy between his puerile dreams and the realities of life, and a victim also of the hypocritical remedy to his moral suffering, now leaves the novel.

Inspector Estival was neither proud nor ashamed of his job. It was his belief that the foundation of all police work was a healthy number of informants, some of whom you pay with money or services, others with voluntary ignorance, this latter category being the most useful along with the third: anonymous sources. In stopping by Antoine Maison's apartment, however, he wasn't hoping to recruit. He was simply going to give his old friend from work a big surprise that, when all was said and done, should be in no way unpleasant. He even smiled as he thought over the encounter, and smiled still more so at the piece of advice he'd been given: "No messing around. There could be some high-class people mixed up in all this. Just do a careful investigation and complete the file. Barbara Durand, daughter of the same Durand who owns all those factories, will somehow be involved. Better to let something go than mess something up." Basically, they'd be delighted if nothing more came out of all this than a harmless discussion. Antoine's welcome was cordial. It'd been a long time since they'd last seen each other, when they were both starting out in the world at Columot's store, and Antoine's assumption was that Estival had come to ask for a favor.

"Well, well, well! What a surprise!"

"Imagine how I feel!"

"How'd you get my address?"

"From the police station."

"The police station?"

"Yeah . . . you didn't hear? . . . I'm an inspector."

"Well, well, congratulations."

Antoine became slightly stiff.

"My old buddy Estival, dropping by to pay me a visit. Or do you prefer Inspector Estival?"

"Come on, Antoine, we're still friends. Anyway, I still consider you mine. And you can even feel good about this, because I have a feeling that I'll be doing you a very big favor, that I'm going to take a thorn about this big out of your foot. So, do you know a certain Artenac?"

"Yes."

"And what about Marie-Louis Arichetti? Raoul Courvoisier, Berthe Cassotte, Jeanne Marjolain, Barbara Durand? Yes, well, you smoke opium with them. I'm not asking you to respond. I'm just telling you what's what. You may or may not know that Artenac was found dead at his house and that he'd been dead for quite a long time . . . a corpse in a complete state of putrefaction. And you may or may not know that word on the street is that his death wasn't normal and that the body may have been transported. Don't look at me like that. I'm not guessing. I know all this. People involved with that junk have big mouths. You all ought to learn how to keep them shut . . . Is it possible that the body was taken in Courvoisier's car and that you went along with him? True or not, you can see that I have very precise information."

"Where'd you hear all that nonsense?"

"Okay, I'll tell you, or rather I'll tell you where it came from. Your buddy Arichetti isn't on the level. People tell him stories and he tells them to people who know what to do with them. You can be sure that we always know about the smalltime dealers. If one's allowed to stay in business, it's because we want him to, and we want him to because he can do favors for us in exchange for the ones we do for him. In fact, since we're already on the subject, do you think you could tell me where Arichetti hangs out?"

"At Charenton, or Ville-Evrard, or some other asylum."

"You aren't going to tell me. Fine, I won't insist. You don't trust me. I think highly enough of you, old friend, not to turn you into an informant."

"I'm happy to hear that. But I'm telling you the truth. Arichetti went crazy. He was committed after being sent to the station infirmary. They found him wandering the streets."

"Well, that's splendid. Seeing as how he was the principal witness, if he's gone crazy my investigation comes to nothing, zilch, zero, and case closed and you're in the clear . . . for now, at least. But it won't always be me looking after your affairs. How long have you been taking it?"

"I don't take it."

"Fine. Understood. But listen to me. If I was a bastard I'd take this little packet from my pocket, go into your bathroom, hide it in the tissue box, and come back in an hour to conduct a search. Do you get it now? Listen. When it comes to drugs, I have them and have nothing to do with them: cocaine, morphine, heroin, opium . . . whatever you want. If you and your little friends want anything, you can get it from me. But listen, Antoine, I don't want to see anyone but you. You're the only one I trust, and it would be very bad for me if word got out about this. Here, five grams of heroin. Get me fifteen francs for each one. You can pay me when you've sold it."

"But buddy . . ."

"I'll see you soon, and not a word about this. If you're not too put off, call me and let's get lunch together. Oh! I almost forgot . . . I'm going to see your friend Courvoisier tomorrow around two thirty. I'd like him to be home. Make sure word gets out about that . . . Keep your chin up, Antoine!"

And he left without listening to anything else Antoine might have had to say.

Antoine informed and reassured Courvoisier, but the latter was unable to hide his fear. The way he saw things, the police could only lead them into a trap. He could hardly believe that such an arrangement existed. Maybe they'd have to pay off the inspector to keep him quiet. Was Antoine sure that he'd admitted nothing, said nothing comprising? That same evening he removed all the material from his home and entrusted it to Columot, keeping only a pellet of opium, which he hid in his watchcase. He then wandered until late in the night from cafés to cinemas, from cinemas to nightclubs.

He wasn't able to fall asleep until dawn. Estival arrived at the expected time. Their conversation was short. The cop simply explained that because of his relationship with Antoine he wouldn't be pursuing the investigation and that Arichetti going crazy was a fortunate turn of events.

After Estival's departure, Courvoisier's mood went from a state of anxiety to one of absolute optimism. He chose an etching from out of a box, which he gave to Antoine as a gift that evening, inviting him to dinner and, afterward, not letting him go home until dawn. Inspector Estival, playing the conscientious civil servant, went back to the station, added several lines to the files for Courvoisier, Arichetti, Berthe, and Jeanne, and, with a sigh, began a new one for his old friend, Antoine Maison.

They'd met through Columot, a storekeeper in the Marais neighborhood. Antoine was eighteen, Estival twenty. Discharged, the latter was working, not without difficulties, as a salesman, whereas his friend was nearing the day when his year would be called up for the draft. In 1918, the war was at full blaze. Throughout the year, Antoine had lived by whatever means possible, taking advantage of any opportunity that came his way, and it was this period of his life that he viewed as the beginning of his adventures. It wasn't without a certain pleasure that he'd met Jacques Columot among Barbara's group of friends . . . Jacques Columot, nephew of father Columot, the aviator whose remarkable exploits and escapades at once incensed and impressed the servile workers of the Columot business. He laughed about it to himself when he returned home at daybreak. He'd said nothing about any of this to Courvoisier. He'd hastily explained that he'd been good friends with Estival before he'd become an inspector, that they'd lost touch, and that the chance of the investigation alone had brought them back together. He said nothing regarding the packet of heroin he'd been given. He'd pay for it in a couple of days and find someone to give it away to. Turning it over on his table, he was tempted to try some. But he wanted to sleep. This need for sleep, which would eventually be his savior, led him into his cool bed like a swimmer into a river. He lay out, stretching his limbs, and drifted off, as straight as an I.

Molinier was a fat man who lived in an immense apartment filled with chinoiseries. Dragons and Buddhas crowded the place's entrance with an attic-like disorder. Entire rooms were filled with piles of prints. Trophies and pieces of armor cluttered the hallways. Rolled up carpets sat in corners. Molinier himself came to open the door. Ruddy-cheeked and dressed in shirtsleeves, he spoke with a reedy voice and with circular gestures. He looked Antoine over before leading him into a backroom.

"A pipe? Sure, what kind do you want? I have some that are quite beautiful and others that are less so."

"Oh, one that looks good but not too ostentatious . . . and in good shape."

"Very good. A pipe for smoking. I know just what you need."

He laid out on the table a dozen or so bamboo pipes, which he'd taken by the handful from a closet. They were simple pipes, with amber or horn tips and saddles made of slightly warped silver.

"If you want my opinion, take this one. It's only three hundred francs and there's at least fifty grams of dross inside of it. As for the bowl . . . good old-fashioned clay's the best, no? Two? Three?"

"Two."

"All right, you already have some for your other pipe. That's to be expected."

His other pipe?

Antoine kept quiet. He didn't dare say that he had no another pipe. Molinier went on:

"A true smoker always has several pipes and a good collection of bowls."

He tied everything up in brown wrapping paper and handed the bundle to his client.

"Oh! Also . . . I'd like some needles . . . three of them."

"Of course."

He stabbed the needles into a cork and handed them over.

Antoine paid, then, before leaving, steeled himself:

"What about opium? Do you have any?"

Molinier smiled contemptuously.

"Absolutely not! There's no risk in handling paraphernalia. I'm an antique dealer, and I only sell authentic pieces. But drugs . . . that's an entirely different kind of business. I'm not trying to end up in prison. Anyway, I think you'll be fine; I'm sure you know where to find some."

Antoine went back down rue de Vaugirard and came out onto avenue de Breteuil. Mademoiselle Muche lived on the fourth floor of a tile-covered country-style house that stood out from the surrounding buildings. Her floor was at the top, below the treetops. The apartment consisted of two rooms. The first, which served as both living room and classroom, was almost entirely taken up by the piano. The second served as kitchen, dining room, and bedroom. Mademoiselle Muche was just as Columot had described her. A black blouse with a stiffened collar rose to her chin. Her small, skinny, wrinkled face was pierced through by two large and astonishingly innocent blue eyes. Jet earrings hung beneath her coiled yellow hair. But her voice was harsh and, at the same time, whimpering. This poor old lady was the physical embodiment of Greed. Her retracted lips, which almost looked as if they'd been swallowed, hinted at unfulfilled desires, vices either struggled against or concealed. Her body emanated an outmoded and tacky perfume that took Antoine back to his childhood and the times he was taken to the houses of unattractive old women whose faces stung him when he had to kiss them. Once again, Antoine felt himself overcome with shyness and a feeling of unfamiliarity. He thought of the ease with which Courvoisier went through life, of Arichetti's blitheness.

"I was sent," he said, "by a friend of mine whom I think you know rather well . . . Mr. Columot."

"Mr. Columot? How is he? Have you come to pick something up for him?"

"No, for myself."

"Ah, for yourself? And how much do you need?"

"Fifty grams."

"Raw or prepared? Prepared, I imagine. I don't sell less than a pound if it's raw. If you were a true smoker you'd prepare it yourself. It's much better. Anyway . . . fifty grams? I don't like to sell such small quantities. How about a hundred? I'll give it to you for four and a half francs instead of five."

She went into the second room and came back carrying an earthenware cream jar with a metal lid, the kind once used in pharmacies. She rolled it inside a newspaper, gave it to Antoine, and showed him to the door.

"Tell Mr. Columot . . ."

Suddenly, she ran to her stove, on which sizzled a spilt liquid. She removed a cover. The smell of fried onions spread through the room . . .

"Tell Mr. Columot that he should come to see me, there's something interesting I'd like to talk to him about."

She opened the door and closed it after her visitor.

It was almost noon. Antoine felt relieved he'd finished his errands. He was filled with a great sense of confidence, as if he'd accomplished some remarkable feat. He decided to have lunch with Estival and called him from a café. Estival answered with a tone that evoked their old friendship and said that he'd wait for him at the office. Antoine jumped in a taxi, overcome by a childlike giddiness at thought of entering police premises with smoking paraphernalia and a hundred grams of opium.

The restaurant looked out over the embankment. The drone of the city was superimposed over the loud sound of passing trucks; the wind blew this sonic mixture over the river, where it blended with the current. Estival was comfortable here. He had, upon entering, shook the hands of several friends and sat down with Antoine at a table near the window. He spoke of the past: the Columot firm where the two of them had met, their Sunday outings spent at cheap restaurants and music hall promenades . . .

"Do you remember all that? . . ."

The memories, however, made Antoine uneasy. They seemed to be part of a life that couldn't have been his. Was it possible that he'd found so much delight in those simple pleasures, the recompense for six days of mediocre work? Was it possible that this young man had been his best friend? The years had drawn an invisible border between them. Antoine had to reflect before speaking to come up with a subject they both could talk about, and he had trouble taking an interest in what his friend had to say. Had he really changed so much? With the exception of his social circle, things were hardly different from how they'd once been. He was still the slave of an uninteresting job and his paltry means of existence. But then, of course, Estival was with the police, which hindered his ability to think or speak. Out of laziness, he took refuge in the past as well, bringing up this accountant, that salesman, this typist.

Him? He must be retired by now. Him? He went to prison for stealing. Him? He's making himself a fair bit of money these days. Her? She's taken a liking to the nightlife . . . The boss? He's dead . . .

But he and Estival wanted to talk about something else. They didn't find the courage to until dessert.

"By the way, I owe you seventy-five francs."

"Oh, really? you sold it . . . Use it to pay the bill . . . And if you need anything else, just let me know."

"Anything else? Oh, I don't think so, you know me, I'm not that interested."

"You say that. But if you need help one day, find me. I'm still your friend. By the way, how's your pal Courvoisier?"

"I think he's doing well. I haven't seen him for a couple of days."

"Yeah. I don't think his business is doing so well. He ought to give up all that nonsense and get down to work. If I was him, I'd be a millionaire. Anyway, that doesn't concern me. And Barbara Durand? There's a pretty girl for you. Berthe Cassotte, too, though she's not quite as attractive. All the same, she's a looker."

Antoine replied halfheartedly. His friends' names, coming from the inspector's mouth, took on the tragic tone of a news story. At least he didn't have to worry about his packages. He could see them on the clothes rack and didn't worry for an instant that Estival would guess what was inside them.

The meal was over. They stood up. Estival held out his hand.

"Well, I'll see you later, old friend, but keep your wits about you. I'll help you out as long as I can, but that won't be forever. And believe me when I say that I have faith in you. One day you'll leave that world behind you . . . although Barbara . . ."

Antoine watched him move off toward place Saint-Michel, where he dissolved into the crowd: one moment he could make out his bright gray hat on the bridge, and the next he was gone. The Seine flowed slowly. On the bank, a fisherman had just caught a fish, which was wriggling at the end of his line and throwing off silver flashes.

Antoine would have been rich had he considered Barbara's love a less vital goal. His youth, his confidence in life and in his own destiny, and his robust health made the material obstacles to his desires only more irritating. Perhaps pride and vanity were mixed up with the passion that drove him. He was poor; he would be rich. He wanted to have Barbara over to his place, that is to say, on his own stage, constructed according to his imagination. Love is the god of hazardous undertakings. He found a new job. He did things that he never would have done for his own satisfaction alone. He found stores of energy inside himself and discovered in his taste for thriftiness, or maybe it should have been called greed, a sense of splendor. He could love money for itself. His love for Barbara allowed him to see it as matériel for war and conquest. His sensuality and his self-indulgence were of great help to him, as was his untapped comedic sensibility. In every man, there's a hidden actor. In moments of loneliness, he told himself beautiful stories similar to the ones he'd heard as a child. He then donned all the typical vestments of heroism and, if he won over Barbara, it wouldn't be by arousing her pity but by earning her admiration. But that which lifted him up was also creating the circumstances for his downfall. Because there's no great captain that doesn't dream of being vanquished. The feminine part of any man can be reduced to servitude by the activity of the masculine. But it's always at risk of reawakening. Caesar must have wished for his murder; Napoleon, for Leipzig and Waterloo. The further he progresses down the path of victory, the more he expects defeat, unconsciously constructing it himself. He was reproducing without realizing it, in his little novel, the deeds and gestures of great men who had reached the realm of mythology after their deaths.

He learned how to dress with taste. He moved and diligently went about finding himself another home. His circumstances didn't allow him to have a lavish abode. Instead, his was charming. Its simplicity came off as intentional. Its very originality suggested a choice determined by money but one that also seemed to be an extension of his imagination. Auportain was helpful in such situations. Inside that selfish old man, with his apparently hardened ways of thinking, was a great reserve of dormant tenderness. The bachelor perhaps regretted not having a son of his own, of leaving behind neither an heir nor a body of work. He knew how to help Antoine choose this or that modest item from a secondhand store, which, in the right frame, could be transformed into a work of art. In the simplicity and youthfulness of Antoine's furnishings, he knew how to add a touch of style, a consistency. Consequently, Antoine had neither a ready-made home nor a masterpiece of design and craftsmanship, but several lovingly self-styled rooms, in which one could imagine him and him alone, a home in which his voice found its proper timbre, in which his friends adapted to Antoine's pitch, to which they didn't come, as if to a theater, to show off their own talents but to sincerely take part in a moment of his life, in the ambience of his company.

Had he been older, Antoine would have constructed a desert around his home to keep unwanted guests at a distance. Those who succeeded in reaching him would have been truly worthy of a visit, would have brought him perfumes and news from far-off places of the planet and of the intellect. But Antoine was young. He couldn't yet dream of taking his pick from the great harvest on offer to him from all quarters. So instead he welcomed everyone, the good and the bad. Then one day, the person for whom he'd built his home came by to see him.

Barbara arrived at around five in the evening, accompanied by Lily. It was June. The windows were open and the birds were singing. Spirits and liqueurs were chilling in ice-filled buckets. Carefully chosen records were waiting beside the phonograph. A cold meal was waiting on a table. The tray, the pipes, the lamp, and the opium composed their still life on a divan near an earthenware salad bowl filled with lemons, cherries, apricots.

Barbara was more attractive than usual, if that was even possible. She borrowed a bathrobe from Antoine and undressed, because her beauty's potential was on full display and she knew how charming a negligee would look on her. Lily did the same, though she was dimly aware that Antoine didn't want her there. She at least knew how to be tactful and, when the warm night air was coming in the through the windows, she quickly smoked several pipes so as to be able to nod comfortably and give the other two their space.

Antoine and Barbara smoked with the tranquility that comes from the knowledge of having an entire night that will be free of any disturbance, of being isolated from the rest of the world, without any reason to worry, in the warmth of springtime. They said little, because Barbara knew full well that her companion would bring up the love he felt for her. And Antoine was indeed waiting to bring this up. But how to say it? A young lover is sincere and lacking in experience. No matter how hard he tries, he can't avoid coming off as preposterous, and all his hope lies in the very charm of his awkwardness. Antoine was neither handsome nor ugly. He didn't know how to stand out. He would need the coaching of a lively social group to feel at ease and to be able to demonstrate that he had as much wit as anyone else. He was quiet by nature, enjoyed solitude as much as the company of others, and was more prone to tenderness than to irony. Unskilled in expressing this tenderness, he also had difficulty letting it show during casual conversation. Not knowing how to protect his feelings, he hid them. But opium, like the Zeitgeist, swathes those who breathe it in. If it's true that there are common features, a shared way of thinking, between the inhabitants of a city or a country because the same oxygen circulates through their lungs, it's even truer that opium unites the minds of smokers spread out around a single lamp. With it one bathes in a thicker atmosphere; it is a gathering in a bed with heavy blankets, an irresistible coupling. This is also perhaps the reason why there are so few solitary smokers: because, despite themselves, they act as spokesmen for their poison. There is, certainly, in every opium addict an unfortunate or unsatisfied lover, a great grandson of Obermann, Adolphe, or René.

Barbara and Antoine's conversation thus grew, as it always did, sentimental, but Antoine had resolved to take it past its usual boundaries. It would be no exaggeration to say that they were intoxicated by their own words. To both of them, their own words seemed more sublime, more moving, more lofty than those of their interlocutor. Because these tormented lovers are also egoists.

Divine words, language of the spheres . . . what would be left of this come sunrise? They'd be unable to remember any of it, and if they were able to remember it their disappointment would only be that much greater.

Barbara and Antoine were engaged less in a conversation than in a series of monologues. Each one followed the current of his or her own mind, connecting it haphazardly to the other's last sentence without taking the time to respond to a question, to link one line of reasoning to another. And so between them the abyss, which they were priding themselves on having eliminated, grew. Distant from one another, they believed themselves to be united, blended, merged into a single being, even though they had abolished the other speaker and projected in their place an embellished version of themselves. They believed themselves to be two, while in reality they were alone, or, perhaps, four: Barbara and Barbara, Antoine and Antoine.

Barbara set the pipe on the tray and lay down on her back, her eyes wide open and fixed on the ceiling. Her throat throbbed. She remained motionless while Antoine lost himself in the lamplight falling over on her skin and the palpitations of her body.

A distant clock rung out. Antoine took Barbara by the wrist.

"Barbara. This can't go on. You know that I love you. Do you love me? I can't stand this game any longer. I can't stand that you're the same with the others as you are with me. I'm telling you: I can't do it anymore. You have to make a decision."

Barbara raised herself up onto her elbow.

"What are you trying to say? There's nothing that needs to stop. I am what I am. I never told you that I would love you. If things can't go on like this, then we'll just have to stop seeing each other!"

Antoine didn't respond. As for Barbara, she may have forgotten what she'd said the very moment she'd uttered her last sentence's final word. They remained motionless at each other's side; then she asked for something to drink. He made tea, squeezed lemons, took cigarettes from a drawer. Lily said something to them from the depths of her divan, on which she'd sunken into a private darkness. She managed to come out of it, smoked several pipes beside them, and then returned to her refuge. Her voice could be heard coming from the shadows for a moment; then she again stopped talking and burrowed into her silence.

Antoine and Barbara fell back into their meditation. The things they said had nothing to do with their true concerns, or rather the former represented the latter to them with so many unconscious precautions that neither Antoine nor Barbara could see through to their secret meaning. But this secret meaning was their invention. She would have liked the chance to respond again to Antoine's question. If he had spoken again of his feelings she would have agreed to give herself to him as a means of consoling her own distress, as an attempt to finally give in to love, because she pitied herself for her own helplessness. From her, he was waiting for the words that would once again permit him to broach the subject of his love. And she thought she could see in him the secret intentions she was hoping for. And he thought that in each one of her words he could detect the beginning of the sentence that would break down the walls that stood between them. Their colloquy continued in this manner, one deceiving the other, while a great wave of fatigue, of weariness, broke over their minds, strangers to the light of the sun, to the general movement of the simple life. They fell silent, watching each other and watching the passing of the hours, waiting for the end of this eternal night, deferring all their hopes to tomorrow while also, out of fear, hoping for tomorrow to be sent into the very distant future, as distant as their own deaths, which seemed to them impossible, as distant as the end of the world, which seemed even more impossible.

Across the three courtyards and the gardens, the sounds of passing cars reached them. Milkmen brusquely set their boxes at the doors of the butter shops. The curtains grew pale. Barbara and

Antoine decided to leave. Lily got up to join them. They opened the windows. Birdsong mixed with the sound of faucets. They delightfully sank their faces into the cool water then, quietly, went down the stairs. The June sun was already shining on the leafy trees. It was four o'clock. The door to the street was open and an elderly ragman was going through the trashcan. Cats approached and, purring, rubbed up against their legs. The ragman, whose profession had habituated him to such encounters, watched them go by without surprise.

They walked down rue Taitbout through a golden light. On boulevard Haussmann, taxis waited in rows. They walked past and followed the streets toward the Opéra. Lily and Antoine had given their arms to Barbara. Intoxicated by the beautiful summer weather, their conversation was disjointed and perfunctory. Via rue de la Paix, they came to place Vendôme. The jewelry shops were closed. The whole neighborhood rested in a peaceful slumber. The road had been recently tarred and the surface was granulating.

"It looks like dross, doesn't it?" said Barbara.

They followed the archways of rue de Castiglione then went past the still-closed Tuileries. Coming to place de la Concorde, but before they'd reached Cours la Reine, the sun, exploding with joyous promise, appeared behind them, as if for the first time ever. The light set aglow the Champs-Élysées, the trees partially shading the street, all the way up to the Arc de Triomphe. At avenue Victor-Emmanuel, Lily left them. For a long while, they could hear her footsteps resounding off the sidewalk.

At place de L'Alma, flowers were being unloaded from cars. The market was being prepared amidst the silent bustle of delivery boys. Quai de Tokyo, awash in light, led them to the gardens of Trocadéro and the Eiffel Tower. They crossed the river. They could hear muffled clangs coming from the train station below, then, not far from the Vélodrome d'Hiver, they discovered a bistro where workers from Citroën were having their breakfast. They went in. The thoroughly washed ground reflected the sunlight. Quickly dissipating steam rose from the coffee machines. The workers hurriedly drank down their coffees with cream, or, more rarely, a coffee spiked with alcohol. Some of them had even ordered Vichy white wine.

"Oh, it's Dondlinger . . . my head plumber," said Barbara.

And she went over to a young man in shirtsleeves who was absorbed in a newspaper. She introduced him to Antoine and, after the three of them had sat down to a table, the café began to empty with the final wails of the factory sirens. On the subway's viaduct, trains went loudly by.

Antoine watched the young man, who, it seemed, was tormented by a desire to speak that was struggling to take shape. He could still feel the previous night enveloping him, weakening him, pushing him toward silence and daydream.

"Do you remember Dondlinger, Antoine? I told you about him."

"Sure, I remember very well. It's surprising we haven't met until now."

"Yes, it is," said Dondlinger, "but I couldn't come the other day. It's always the same. Whenever I want to do something, my mom gets sick. It's like she can sense my plans and decides to catch something. What would you do if you were me? You'd turn yourself into a nurse. But what can I say? I've never had much luck. Anyway, there'll be another time, won't there, madame Barbara?"

"What about Saturday, in the evening? That way you can look forward to a calm Sunday and not worry about having to go to work."

"Oh, work, it's not too busy at the moment . . . toilets burst, sinks get clogged. You can't imagine what people get stuck in their sinks. I'm not talking about hair, no, sometimes you pull out an entire wig. And all kinds of other crazy things. Listen to this. One time, at some old hag's house, I found a thousand-franc bill, that's right, a thousand francs torn up and turned into a bung. I put it back together and took it to the bank for a replacement. That doesn't happen too often, but there's all sorts of other things. Rings, even wedding rings. How can someone lose their wedding ring in a sink? Of course, there's the plug that covers the drainage hole. But when the chain breaks, everything ends up falling inside. Fortunately there's the bend, where everything gets stuck. But still, I don't understand how the charming old thing could block hers with a thousand franc bill. Another love story, you can bet your life on that. The well-to-do get themselves into some serious arguments, and when they do you can be sure someone will end up doing something idiotic. It's the same with tubs. You think to yourself: a bath, it's just water and soap. Well, things really aren't that simple. I once saw a tub clogged with jam and foie gras. And that's not even the worst of it. People do everything you can imagine and then some in their bathtubs. People? They're pigs when you see what's inside their pipes."

Barbara was laughing. He emphasized the point:

"That's right, madame Barbara, pigs, and bathrooms are their trashcans."

He stood up.

"I've got to get going. I'll see you on Saturday, madame Barbara. You as well, sir. As for me, I'm off to scrub the pipes. A dirty job, in a dingy house. Pigs, just like the others."

And with that, he left.

"Is that how you imagined my plumber, Antoine?"

"A little. Anyway, he's funny."

"You'll see on Saturday. But let's get back. It's nine, and I want to sleep."

He accompanied Barbara to her door and, before leaving, they exchanged a passionless, reserved, subdued kiss. She went quickly inside, disappointed to see him stay out on the street and not try to follow her in.

Seated across from him, Auportain had patiently listened to Courvoisier's speech. It was settled. He was once and for all turning his back on drugs.

"When I think of all the lost time! For three years I've had all the notes relating to my research on cosmic rays and a big manuscript almost ready for printing set aside in a drawer. It's a book on the evolution of hypothesis in physics since Descartes, a fascinating subject, a book that once filled me with hope and kept me going forward. It was the key to my future work. Believe me, my dear Auportain, I am a man, a real man, with willpower, drive, and a strong stomach. I've set myself a deadline. In six months, all of my work needs to be brought up to date, and finished as well. A lot of things have happened in physics over the past three years. In half a year, everything will be with the publisher, and as for myself, I'll be far away from the opium dens, spending entire days in the laboratory. I need to get clean. Of that I'm sure. It's what I want."

"Check yourself into a recovery home."

"No, that's for the weak willed. I want to work, and it's important that I start working right away. Besides, I need money."

"You don't go about getting clean all by yourself. It doesn't matter how determined you are. In a clinic, however, you're guaranteed to get clean. Afterward, it's your job not to fall back into it.

If you make it that far, you'll already have a reason to be proud of yourself. But it's one person out of a hundred that doesn't go back to the pipe or the syringe."

"But I swear to you . . ."

"Don't swear on anything. I've heard thousands of vows from drug addicts! And never have I seen one kept."

"I'm begging you, Auportain, help me."

"Help you what? I'd barely have my back turned before you called your friends asking them to bring you your trash. And what power do I have over you? I'm an addict myself and I plan on remaining one."

"But how do you do it, how do you live a normal life?"

"I have a great taste for virtue and lots of luck. I belong to a rare category of people."

"Tell me how it's done and I'll do it."

"You could try the Chinese bottle. How much opium do you take a day?"

"I don't smoke anymore. It took too much time. I eat it, or sometimes drink it."

"How much per day?"

"I've gone down a lot. A gram."

"Let's say five grams then, and I'm almost certainly underestimating. If I were a doctor, you would have lied in the other direction and said ten grams.

"You go get a carafe or a magnum of champagne. Then you measure how many port glasses it holds. I don't know the exact number, but let's say forty. You dissolve two hundred grams of drug inside of it. Every day you drink a glass, but each day you replace what you drank with the same quantity of pure water. Your solution will gradually grow weaker and soon, without even realizing it, you'll be drinking pure water . . . in theory."

"That's fantastic! There's Chinese ingenuity for you. Thanks for the recipe . . ."

"Not so fast . . . I said in theory. I've explained the system to you, for what it's worth. But I don't believe in its effectiveness."

"Well, I do. You'll see . . ."

"That's all I'm asking for."

Immediately after their conversation, Courvoisier went to buy a magnum of Cliquot and invited Berthe over to drink it. It was a sentimental evening. Courvoisier was radiant with optimism and enthusiastic again about life and what the world had to offer.

"What about you, my little Berthe? Don't you think it's a shame to see each other the way we do, never lucid, never sure about one another. At your age, as beautiful as you are, it's such a waste to stay shackled to the pipe. We're crazy for not paying more attention to you, you, Lily, Jeanne and Noëlle and Marie-Jacqueline and Barbara . . ."

"Well, it seems to me that you pay close enough attention to all of them . . . what about Barbara!"

"No, that's just an act. Alone, we're always alone, and whatever kisses we exchange never mean anything, never lead to anything. Love among us? No. Just selfishness. Do you know what we're like? Pederasts. We form a secret, international society, just like them, recognizing each other through the obvious but indescribable signs. In every country around the world we know that we can find other people just like us; we have our own underworld and high society, our heroes and our criminals; and, like pederasts, we drag around our defects, our lies, our impotence, our cowardice, our moral, sometimes physical, filth. Ah, where is it, our first pipe, or rather the second . . . the dream multiplied, the genie within mouth's reach . . . And what has this genie ever produced? Might as well kill yourself and be done with it."

"Or die young, like Artenac."

"Artenac . . . Do you think that foolish death of his was written out in his destiny? No. Nothing noble or tragic about it . . . Just foolishness, without any greater meaning. Only teenagers believe in the poetry and romanticism of drugs. At least the little hookers who stuff their nostrils aren't debasing themselves any further by taking it. But us! I can't even look at myself in the mirror anymore. It takes the soul of a whore to put up with the life we're living. I'm such an idiot! My sweet Berthe . . . I love glory, I love wealth, I love life. Can you tell me how I got into this mess? I'm punishing myself, depriving myself of all the things I love . . ."

"Love?"

"Yes, love. Berthe, you're a big boy like me. Let's leave all this behind and rediscover our freedom. Get clean with me. You can come over each day to drink a glass from the magnum. Or if you want, I can leave it at with you and I'll come over to your place. And then, Berthe, with each other's help, don't you think it's possible for the two of us to find happiness?"

Berthe let herself get caught up in his thinking.

"We could travel. You're right. It's stupid to waste your youth. I also like luxury, nice dresses, parties."

"When should we start? right away? or maybe not . . . tomorrow. Let this be the last evening of our lunacy."

The magnum was empty. The last drops of champagne bubbled in their glasses like a message of joy. They measured the water together, weighed the opium, dissolved the latter in the former. There was still opium left in the jar.

"Let's finish it," proposed Berthe, "seeing how this is our last night."

And, again, they settled themselves on the divan, with all the familiar motions, with the lacquerware tray, the needles, the pipe, and the lamp, which was soon flickering in the darkness. Their sentimental dialogue lasted until the morning. They fell asleep in each other's arms and woke up late. Berthe got out of bed to make tea and toast, then, since the day was already advanced, they put off the start of their cure until the following day. Again, they smoked. Then Berthe left. It was six in the evening. They'd planned to meet each other the next morning at her apartment. She took the big bottle with her, and they exchanged a long kiss on the landing.

The next day, Courvoisier slept in late, and the afternoon was already well-advanced when he arrived at Berthe's. He could smell the familiar fragrance from the door. She was already smoking with Noëlle.

"I waited for you, but you didn't come. Noëlle came over and she didn't have anything. I thought you'd changed your mind and that we'd start tomorrow. And since I couldn't wait, we smoked. Anyway, we just started."

"No, I didn't change my mind. I was just tired . . ."

He didn't have the energy to reproach her and, since everything was ready, he smoked as well.

He spent the rest of the night at Berthe's, so they could start the cure in the morning. At eight o'clock, he woke up and noted to himself that the opium solution was an excellent aperitif. The two of them had breakfast together before going their separate ways. He wanted to work. He went back home and took his notes out from their drawer. The first hour was exhilarating. He again felt the familiar zeal from his years of work, and he reread certain sentences with a profound sense of pleasure. Some of his observations seemed full of promise, rich with potential.

Then he took out a package of scientific journals, and his optimism quickly went to pieces. While he'd been wasting his time, others had been working. He found his name cited several times in some of the oldest volumes, but, soon, overtaken and forgotten, he could no longer find that assemblage of letters whose familiar architecture formed the facade of his ego. He began arranging the journals. It wasn't long before he understood, however, that all his work was dated and that he'd now have to become the student of people he should instead have been teaching. Every unknown name that he found at the bottom of an intriguing article was a fresh wound to his ego. He abandoned this task to look over his manuscript on hypotheses. But his own writing was unintelligible to him. Moreover, and without being fully conscience of it, he was suffering physically. A heaviness in his stomach was making it difficult to breathe, and his eyes soon began to water. Most noticeably, a fear, an anxiety, a feeling of catastrophe was looming over him. He mechanically read and reread a sentence while an interior dream twisted around lugubrious draperies. He sneezed several times in a row and thought that maybe he'd caught a cold during the night. Meanwhile, his sense of discomfort increased. It was the time of day when he'd normally be smoking a succession of pipes. He knew that he shouldn't smoke now. But a tingling sensation had come over him. It began with an itching in his back, which then spread to the tips of his fingers and the palms of his hands and, finally, to the rest of his body. He lit a cigarette. The smoke tasted bitter. A pain in his stomach caused him to double over. He was still tearing up. He blew his nose several times and, realizing that his hand was wet, saw that he was drooling. A wave of irritation swept over him. Everything had taken on an air of hostility: the creases in the pillow beneath the back of his neck, the cigarette turning to ash, the sounds from the street, even the air entering his lungs. Evening was falling. He felt lost in the depths of the city, utterly abandoned. His friends' names annoyed him when they crossed his mind. He felt a rage raising up against them, against their images, their words, even the sound of their voices, and a nauseating stream of distant grievances flowed by in his mind.

As evening set in, it became intolerable. He took out his pipe and scraped the bowl to collect the dross. He looked for more on the tray, on the needles, even on the lamp, where it was soaked in oil. Then he was overcome with anger. He broke the pipe and the lamp, lit a fire, and threw the debris inside it, along with the arduously collected dross. He shuddered. He put more wood in the fireplace and settled morosely beside it. Then he started to cry. The tears helped. He poured himself a large glass of cognac, which he drank straight down, then another, and then he fell asleep on the couch.

When he woke up, it was night. The fire had gone out and he was cold. He wanted to turn on the light but struggled to find the switch. When he could see clearly he looked over his haggard face and its three-day-old beard. His hands were shaking.

He drank more cognac, then, suddenly, left for Berthe's.

Barely out into the street, he felt a streak of pain shoot through this stomach. He went into a café and thought he might faint. When he came back out, his longing for the drug was so strong that he would have happily killed someone for it. In a taxi, his feverish impatience grew still more acute. He rushed up the stairs to Berthe's. When she opened, surprised, her rested face lit up with a smile that seemed to be mocking him. He went into the apartment, poured himself a large glass of the opiate-laced solution, and collapsed, trembling, onto a couch.

"What's wrong with you? You're pale as a ghost."

"And you? you're just fine? You haven't been suffering without the drug?"

"No."

"Well then! Did you smoke? . . ."

"Oh! just one or two little pipes. It doesn't make any difference."

"Doesn't make any difference! If you hadn't smoked them you'd see what kind of difference it makes. In any case, you're not going to get clean with one or two little pipes."

"You're becoming as insufferable as Auportain."

"All right. I think I'd be better off getting clean by myself. I thought you'd be able to handle it."

"You must be joking. Have you been able to handle it? You should have seen the state you were in when you got here, and what about that glassful you had. You didn't even take the time to say hello."

And it was that very glassful that was now taking effect and soothing the pain; Courvoisier had rediscovered in the bosom of his vice an artificial equilibrium. He was inclined to feel as compassionate for her as he did for himself.

"We don't need to turn this into some kind of tragedy. We'll both have to put up with nervous outbreaks before this is all over. We have to help each other, not bicker and squabble. How could I have told Auportain that a gram a day would be enough! He said five grams, and even that's not enough."

"Maybe we should have one glass in the morning and one in the evening."

"At that rate the diminution of the dosage would be too much. Imagine having to put four glasses of water back into the bottle: a tenth of the total. Maybe it'd be better if we each had our own."

And that was how they proceeded. But, after several days, they could no longer maintain their discipline. Each day, they broke their rule. Each day, the drug grew stronger. They could feel it triumphing over their desire for health, over their willpower.

Berthe went back to the pipe and to the evenings spent at friends' apartments. So did Courvoisier. But he didn't replace his burnt, shattered pipe. Heroin took over the role that opium had once played in his life and, consequently, the little tins with the picturesque labels were replaced by white paper packets. His notes, his manuscripts, lingered for a while out in the open before being returned to their drawer, where they would, in all likelihood, remain.

Moreover, money was beginning to become a source of concern. He'd squandered his small inheritance, and he now had to sell beloved books, jewels, paintings. He was able to keep up appearances for a while. He knew how to hide his problems. But each new day was more distressful than the last, and he would find himself thinking over all the lost time, which only went on growing. In vain, he would pledge to make a change the next day. He wasn't ready yet to admit that this was something he was incapable of and that immediate need was the only thing that drove him, that in reality he was struggling just to make it from one day to the next.

Auportain never asked him about his plan. In any case, he was well informed enough to know that it had failed, if in fact it'd ever actually been attempted.

One day, however, Courvoisier alluded to their discussion.

"Between you and me, my dear Auportain, the Chinese disappoint me. That famous bottle of theirs is a joke."

"Don't blame the Chinese. I don't think they had anything to do with that shrewd little invention. Actually, I think it was a naval officer who first came up with it."

Barbara, thanks to her fortune, always had a well-stocked and continuously replenished supply of drugs, which would have allowed her to go several months without having to buy more. And because of this same fortune, she knew that she was safe from police searches. But even if addicts distrust one another, even if they're prone to betrayal and compulsive lying, it's still quite rare for them not to help each other in cases of shortage. Barbara had lent opium to Columot when he didn't have any, to Courvoisier when he didn't have money to buy any, to Marie-Jacqueline when her dealer had been arrested. Lily had gone through her reserve of heroin and one day found herself unable to smoke her daily dose. She instinctively distrusted and thus avoided the smalltime dealers, putting all her confidence in the big traffickers, similar to how she refused to wear anything that didn't come from luxury fashion designers. But addicts' precautions tend to fall apart as easily as their little oaths to stop using. Only Auportain, thanks to his self-proclaimed lack of generosity, was never at risk of finding himself without drugs. He had firmly resolved to veil the twilight of his life in opium smoke. As for the others, they combined their distrust and greed with an insouciance and profligacy reminiscent of a child who thinks the opened jar of jam will last for months. Moreover, they were victims of their mood. When it tilted them toward confidence and optimism, they would have happily handed away the last of their francs. On the contrary, when suffering from the attack of depression that proceeds the moment when smoking or snorting becomes an imperious necessity, they would have defended with their lives whatever supply of heroin or opium they had in their possession.

Lily had begun dedicating the remaining powers of her charm to her vice, and knew the best times to beg from Barbara. The others did as well, or perhaps it was simply that their voices tended to come through the telephone right when her solitude and its attendant silence were reaching a point of intolerability. Perhaps it was even because of them that Barbara was able to escape her obsessive thoughts of suicide. Perhaps they'd come themselves to bring a reassuring presence into that solitude.

Barbara called Antoine. He brought her the bag of heroin bought from Estival, which allowed her to enjoy several worry-free days. Then she again found that her supply was running low. She consequently pestered Antoine, who, over the course of two weeks, managed to find sufficient quantities by going to suspect dealers. He at first tried to get in touch with Estival, but he was away on an investigation. Then he went around to bars and dance clubs, sometimes not finding what he was looking for until very late at night. Afterward, he'd take it to Barbara's, where he'd wait for daybreak engrossed in sentimental conversations that left him more intoxicated than the drugs.

One day, however, he was unable to find anything. Barbara's disappointment turned quickly to anger, and Antoine walked home after silently departing.

Barbara tried to contact Columot. He made sure that she was told he wasn't available, knowing full well what was wanted of him and promising to himself that he'd pay back his debts, not with money, which mattered little to Barbara, but in kind. As for Courvoisier, he was off traveling. Lily, giving into a wrongheaded impulse, went to see her. Barbara demanded heroin so aggressively from her that their conversation devolved into an argument. What's more, Lily had once again come to borrow money. She thought she'd extinguished her friend's anger by asking for it, but Barbara was already suffering from withdrawal. She attacked Lily with a vigor and treacherousness that infuriated her, piling insult upon insult. They both reproached the other for the favors they'd done each other. Then, the moment the argument was on the verge of turning into something even worse, they parted ways. Alone again, Barbara went to the window and cried as she looked out over Paris. She imagined throwing herself off the balcony and falling endlessly over the city, her tragic death leading her into a definitive sleep. Several hundred meters away, Lily, leaning on a parapet along the embankment, was crying and watching the progression of the Seine, in which, if only she could find the courage, she would have liked to settle permanently.

This was where Dondlinger found her. He understood only one thing from her disorderly explanation, which was that Barbara was unhappy. Being too much in love with Barbara to concern himself with any other woman, he gave scant attention to Lily's lamentations. He hurried to her house, where she embraced him feverishly and begged him to find her drugs, any drugs, whatever the cost. The conversation was delightful for Dondlinger and dramatic for Barbara, who clung to him as if he were a lifebuoy. Dondlinger was ecstatic. The time he'd spent with her had at first been an enchantment, but he'd soon begun to suffer from the obstacles that had risen up between him and his dream. He'd soon suspected that it'd all been nothing but a whim. But, at that moment, he understood that luck had finally come his way. He promised everything and more and went away saying that he'd be back by evening.

Dondlinger set out, drunk with boldness and the promises he'd made. When he found himself back out in the streets, Paris suddenly seemed larger than the Sahara, a vast place in which he had to find, buried somewhere in the sand, a needle or a coin. He had only five francs on him. He went into a small bar and quickly spent them on four glasses of brandy. The low-quality alcohol hastened him outside and, without a plan, he started making his way through the streets, where a light rain made him smell like a wet dog. He walked fast, child of the countryside that he was, used to crossing streets and intersections in the same way that a peasant in pursuit of a hare tramps through a field. He suddenly found himself before the black hole, glittering with lights, of place de l'Étoile. Following boulevard de Courcelles, he went to place Clichy. It would soon be nine. Bob, his old friend who worked as a porter in a nightclub, should have already been at work. He saw him from the top of rue Fontaine, in front of the club, talking with the taxi drivers. His greeting was cordial but, in Dondlinger's eyes, somewhat pretentious.

"There you are, Toto, you've come at a good time. I've just gotten off. Come knock back a drink or two next door. How's it going? Everything good?" Then, in the light of the café: "Good God! Where are you coming from? Don't have any cash to take the subway? In weather like this, I always take a cab. Better warm yourself up. Have a sportbeef, with a drop of white wine."

Without asking anyone, he took a buttered slice of bread from a pyramid-shaped stack in a saucer on the counter and dipped it into his cup.

"Eat. It's important to eat. Have a sandwich. Miss, a sausage sandwich, and a ham sandwich, too. Eat already! Miss, this is all on me. Can you wait just a quick second? I'll be right back."

He left then returned.

"Ought to drink, too. Miss, a glass of white wine. Say, you don't seem to be doing so well. Here, take this."

And he slid two one-hundred-franc bills into Dondlinger's hands.

Dondlinger rediscovered a sense of equilibrium.

"Listen, there's something else. I need heroin."

"Ah, shit, what's gotten into you? What the hell do you need it for?"

"It's for my girl. A rich girl. Yeah, that's right. Don't laugh, I'm not joking. She's a respectable woman. I wouldn't dare ask her for money. Do you get it? She needs it, and if she doesn't get it she'll die."

"Well damn, it sounds like you've let yourself become a john. What are girls for if you can't get any money out of them?"

"I'm crazy about her!"

"Idiot. That's even worse. How do you expect her to respect you if she doesn't pay? And you really think she can't tell you're broke from the way you dress? Anyway, that's your business."

"Do you know where I can find it?"

"If you'd come last week, you could have had it in five minutes. But they've taken in a bunch of dealers these past couple of days. Snitches, every last one of them. So I don't know anymore. There's Marco, but I don't want to get myself too involved . . . one second."

He left again and came back with a pale, well-dressed, gray-eyed individual, who ordered a quarter-liter of Vittel. Bob went on:

"Well, the guy's got nothing. He stashed everything away. But he says you can go to see Fernand, at the hôtel de Kharbine. You can tell him that Jean sent you. Do you know the way? It's nearby, rue de Clichy."

Dondlinger set out again. He found the hotel and went up a warm stairwell with worn carpeting and a banister that was sticky with polish. He knocked on the designated door. There was a long silence, then the door half-opened and a head appeared. It belonged to tall guy in pink pajamas with messy black hair falling over his face. Upon hearing the name Jean, he showed the visitor into a bedroom lit by a small lamp. The curled-up body of a woman could be discerned in the bed, her hair spilling out past the sheet.

Dondlinger explained his reason for coming.

"Oh, nothing to be done about that. I've got nothing left. Everything's stashed away. Things have taken turn for the worse and I'm marked. But you can go to the Halles, rue Rambuteau. Go into a café on the right and ask for Alfred. The café's also called Alfred, Chez Alfred. Tell him that I sent you. But get a move on, it's best that you're not seen hanging around here."

Dondlinger hailed a taxi at la pointe Saint-Eustache. He found Alfred's café and then Alfred, fat and chubby-cheeked with droopy eyelids, who was playing cards in a back room. Hearing Fernand's name, he got up and led the young man outside.

"How much do you need?"

"It depends on the price."

"Thirty francs."

"Okay, then five, or, no, six."

"That's good. Give me a hundred and seventy five francs, then go to the Halles metro station at eleven thirty. It's over there, do you see it? Don't get worried if there's other people around, they're just customers. There'll be two women and a car, a big Talbot. See you soon!"

It was a quarter past ten. Dondlinger had some fifteen francs left. He stopped by the grill on the corner of rue Montorgueil and ate a vinegar-soaked sausage in a piece of bread then had a coffee next door. But he couldn't keep still. He walked through the pavilions and the surrounding area, where pyramids of turnips and carrots formed harmonious patterns of red and green or white and green beneath the color-enhancing glare of the tall streetlights. The quarter hour sounded at Saint-Eustache as he started toward the metro station with a not fully acknowledged fear of having been cheated. At the corner of rue Mondétour, he suddenly bumped into Alfred, who was lighting a cigarette.

"Well, since you're here, here's the goods."

He handed over a package, which Dondlinger hid in his pocket. With great strides Alfred walked toward the station's entrance. Dondlinger followed, but did so slowly in order not to disturb him.

He watched Alfred approach a group of shadowy figures. The rain, which hadn't let up, caused the actors to blur into the scenery. Suddenly, four men got out of a taxi. There was a commotion. A whistle was blown. Six agents lying in wait rushed forward to help. Without quite understanding what was going on, Dondlinger watched the scene unfold. Then everything calmed down. The group split up. Some got into the Talbot; others were climbing into the taxi when a voice cried out:

"The young gentleman over there, under the streetlight, arrest him, too. He was talking to him just a minute ago."

Dondlinger realized they were talking about him and began running in the opposite direction. He heard the heavy steps of two officers coming from behind him. He turned into a maze of narrow streets, finding himself time and time again in the same places, turning and turning around but never losing his pursuers. Suddenly a firefighter's horn rang out and a large red car almost crushed him. There was a series of jumbled noises and then suddenly he found himself alone and out of breath on place des Victoires. He started off again along the darkest roads he could find and finally came to a metro station. On the platform he fell onto a bench, his temples throbbing and his mouth filled with saliva.

When he arrived at Barbara's, she was lying down, smoking opium with Columot, who'd miraculously arrived earlier in the evening. Barbara greeted Dondlinger flatly. She took the drugs from him, put them in a drawer, and invited him to smoke without bothering to ask if she owed him money or if he'd had any trouble getting the heroin.

Dondlinger felt outside of the conversation, as if he'd been invited out of pity. He considered leaving but couldn't work up the courage to do so. He smoked greedily and got lost in a melancholic dream world, which he didn't come out of until morning, when Columot offered to drop him off somewhere. Columot was naturally charming, but more than anything else he loved to be liked, he loved to charm. He knew what to say to Dondlinger, how to earn his trust, how to listen to him.

And Dondlinger recounted the events of his night.

"I imagine you were disappointed when you arrived and saw that Barbara no longer needed you and that so many risks had been taken for nothing."

"Why?"

"I don't know, but that was my feeling. An adventure like that's exciting. When your heart starts racing . . . and Barbara didn't even ask you what had happened."

"She couldn't have known."

"She couldn't have cared less about knowing. For her, life is very simple. I bet she didn't even pay you back for the drugs. Tell me how much she owes you; I'll pay for them. Don't worry, I'll get it back from her. It'll be easy enough for me. While you, well, you wouldn't dare bring it up."

"No, please, it's fine."

"I insist. Come on, we'll settle this over a drink."

He stopped his car in front of the New-York Bar, rue Daunou, and led his companion into what was for him a new world. The place was dark but cheerful. Above the bar hung an enormous pair of boxing gloves, which had once belonged to Carnera. On the wall, caricatures by Sem. In a cabinet, dusty bottles of whiskey and gin. Some Americans were playing dice on the bar and laughing like children.

"They have the best whiskey in Paris here. It's better than that trash of a drug, as Auportain would say."

They were served a golden alcohol that sparkled with soda.

More customers had just come in, trading big slaps on the shoulders while exchanging their first smiles of the day.

"Listen, Barbara's like every other woman. It's only natural for her to get whatever she wants. What would be extraordinary for her, and even unjust, would be an obstacle, a rebuff. You shouldn't ask from her more than she can give: her beauty, her whim, and her cheerfulness! And be careful about getting down over her. Anyway, I'm not sure why I'm saying all this to you. We're all the same. Here, old pal, five hundred francs. Take it without regret, without hesitation, as something from one friend to another."

Dondlinger felt himself go warm with amity. He didn't refuse the large bill. The whiskey had gone to his head. He became talkative, told stories from his life, opened his heart to the other.

Columot was touched. The man sitting on the other side of the table was always his best friend, even if he forgot about him the moment they parted ways.

He took Dondlinger to eat at the Cercle des Armateurs du Littoral, or the Littoral as the regulars called it, a gambling den set up in the former apartments of the Duke of Brunswick. In return for several lost hands of baccarat, you could have lunch and dinner for free. The food was good. Columot had already shown the place to Antoine; they found him at a table, sitting before a dozen hors d'oeuvres.

"Antoine, my dear, life is beautiful, our health is good, and Dondlinger here is a great guy. Let's eat, let's eat, I'm hungry and I'm happy to see you."

Columot wasn't mean spirited, but he liked to talk when he was in a good mood and couldn't help but allude to Dondlinger's infatuation with Barbara. Antoine went immediately on the defensive. He considered Dondlinger all the more threatening as a rival given the fact that he was, by all appearances, a less formidable one. A daydreamer when alone, always lost in triumphant reveries that opium, when he took it, had little effect on, he was also often beset by suspicion and discouragement. The sensitivity peculiar to people in love also made him dimly aware that Dondlinger had gotten further than he had, that his simplicity and his straightforward, sometimes even awkward, behavior were in fact advantages that he himself, who carefully thought through every action and who, because of his prudence, became timid, lacked. And so this faculty of imagination that protected him from danger, and that would go on protecting him still, was also an obstacle in his pursuit of happiness. He felt a tinge of melancholy while thinking this over and, even though he was made for taking in the light of spring and summer, reveled in a gray-skied season that his health, his self-confidence, however hidden it might have been, and his luck, because he certainly had it, still managed to fill with light.

Dondlinger vaguely sensed that some cloud had intruded upon the pleasant day, even though Antoine and Columot were outwardly behaving the same. The conversation was light-hearted, but he felt someone's suspicion and enmity weighing on him.

The meal came to an end. Columot sat down at the baccarat table and threw down several *louis* with that typical ease of his, intimidating to Dondlinger, a cause of envy for Antoine. The other two went down the stairs together and parted ways on the street.

In Marie-Jacqueline's little apartment, Simonne, Berthe, and Dondlinger stood cramped in the kitchen watching Courvoisier prepare the dross. He'd scraped the bowls and the interiors of the pipes, the surfaces of the trays, the bottoms of the medicine jars that had once held the drug. The collection of residue was dissolving in a pot of boiling water, into which he'd also put the silver needles. He brought them out shiny and hot. A strong smell wafted through the room, and they took it in with delight.

"It won't be much more than dross of dross, but it's all we have until Auportain gets here and it'll make the wait easier."

Nobody said anything in response. They could hear a fine rain falling behind the shutters and from time to time heavier drops crashing down onto the balcony. The liquid was growing thicker. This was the moment that required the most delicacy. If the drug were overcooked it would become too thick, if it were undercooked it would be too thin. Courvoisier enjoyed being watched. He was proud of his preparatory talents and childishly bound his honor to the operation's success. Finally, he turned down the gas, poured the mixture into a jar, threw out several insoluble pieces of residue, and concluded the operation by putting the precious receptacle into a bain-marie. The water simmered for several more minutes, then settled. It was ready. The evening began as so many others had, even if they now smoked a thicker and bitterer paste, which dried the throat, than they were accustomed to. Around ten o'clock, they'd used up the final drops.

"This stuff is really trash," said Marie-Jacqueline. "I'll clean the materials so Auportain's *real* opium doesn't get ruined."

She went about the task with all the fervor of a housewife polishing her pots and pans, and her activity augmented her friends' torpor. When she'd finished, she arranged everything on a chest of drawers and served tea with lemon slices. They drank. Courvoisier had opened the window and was watching for Auportain. A taxi stopped in front of the building. The young man closed the casement.

"He's here."

The doorbell rang. Marie-Jacqueline went to open it. They heard a commotion, heavy steps, protests from the young woman. The bedroom door opened and two officers entered with an inspector.

"I don't think there's any point in denying it, is there?" he said. "Ladies, gentlemen, hand over your drugs and let's settle this without any fuss."

Courvoisier was composed.

"Settle what? What drugs?"

"Don't deny it! You can smell it from the street."

"We have no idea what you're talking about."

"What about all this?" he said, pointing to the pipes, the trays set on the chest of drawers. "You use that to make jam, I suppose?"

"Those are pieces of art, curiosities. Simply owning a Chinese pipe doesn't mean you smoke opium."

"How would you feel about me taking a look through the place?"

"Look all you want."

The inspector began his search. It was easy: the scantily furnished apartment consisted of a single room, a small bathroom, a small kitchen, and an entryway. He went through the furniture, checked the feet of the chest of drawers and the couch, the seams of the fitted carpet. He emptied the pockets of the clothes found in a closet, lifted several paintings, checked the gas pipes, and, standing on top of a stool, used his flashlight to illuminate the toilet tank.

"I know there are drugs here. Are you going to hand them over or would you rather I take you down to the station and search you there?"

"Do what you have to do."

Courvoisier's confidence reassured the others. The inspector gave the smoking materials to an officer, who then led the others outside, before leaving in turn and closing the door behind him.

Out on the sidewalk, the wet air washed over their faces. Their nervousness made them feel like laughing, but they kept quiet. The two officers, Berthe, and Dondlinger got into the taxi. The inspector hailed another and climbed in with Simonne, Marie-Jacqueline, and Courvoisier. As the two taxis started off, a third stopped in front of the neighboring building. Its occupant walked toward the door, appeared to hesitate, and then went to ring the bell at the house which the little convoy had just come out of. It was a tardily arrived Auportain. It was after midnight. The two cars were already going around the corner of the next street and, before entering, he absentmindedly glanced at their taillights and the reddish hue they gave off from behind the curtain of rain.

Auportain went up the stairs, rang, and, when no one answered, took the key from beneath the carpet. He went in, turned on a light, approached the fire. He was only half-surprised by the absence of Marie-Jacqueline and his friends. Probably they'd gone out for a quick drink. The presence of the key in its usual hiding place, the unlocked door, suggested that they'd be back soon. He rekindled the fire and served himself a glass of still warm and very strong tea, into which he squeezed some lemon juice. While smoking a cigarette, he got lost in the usual thickets of his dream world. He was enjoying his solitude and the feeling of unfamiliarity in this apartment that was comfortable but not at all to his taste. It wouldn't be long, some ten or so years at most, before the style he preferred existed only in the domain of images, museums, and recreation. Maybe one day the pieces of furniture he loved and among which he went about his life with so much security would serve as the decor for other lives, other romances, other sorrows. Marie-Jacqueline's furniture, her knick-knacks, her paintings would, in their own turn, undergo a similar process. Auportain felt older from the centuries to come than from the past years he'd lived through and even, at certain moments, he believed, lived intensely. The tick-tock of the clock was soon in sync with the rhythm of his breathing and pulse. The little steady beats knocked on invisible doors. He checked his watch, shrugged his shoulders. He'd been waiting for an hour and a half. His smile was half-sorrowful, half-ironic, and he put a large log on the embers. He drank another glass of tea, which was now completely cold, then set, in a conspicuous place on the chest of drawers, a tin of opium from the Indochinese Régie, turned out the light, left, put the key back in its place . . . Outside, the rain had stopped, but the streetlights still reflected off the wet asphalt. He went to the left, in the direction of the nearest taxi station. If, after walking several hundred meters, he'd turned round, he would have seen a set of shadowy figures get out from two cars that had stopped in front of Marie-Jacqueline's building.

The obstinate inspector led the whole group back into the apartment. Nothing had convinced him of their innocence, not the search, nor the examination of the carefully washed materials, nor the denials of the accused. He was sure there was opium somewhere and he was determined to find it. Reaching the landing, he told them to wait and went to check the bathroom and entryway to make sure there were no other possible hiding places. Then he made them go in with the two officers, had them sit down, and, in the presence of Courvoisier, began a second examination of the apartment. He methodically knocked along the walls and, through the fitted carpet, on the floorboards. He went over the couch, spent a long time feeling the cushions and pillows, searched the windowsills and the gutter, emptied out the chest of drawers. In the kitchen, he likewise inspected anything that might contain drugs. At last, clearly irritated, he opened the door:

"You've got me this time, but I promise that we'll meet again. Goodbye, you're free to go."

"And what about the art pieces you took?" asked Courvoisier.

"You can get them from the station tomorrow."

"You could have at least brought them back. What a way to behave!"

The inspector didn't respond. He furiously called to the officers:

"Are you coming or what?"

They listened to their footsteps grow quiet on the stairwell and Simonne fell onto the couch, laughing sharply.

"Do you realize what a catastrophe it would have been if Auportain had come while we were gone?" exclaimed Courvoisier.

"Auportain is splendid, even when he stands you up. But what do we do now?" asked Simonne. "It's two in the morning!"

"It is, and we don't have any drugs."

"We could call Auportain."

"Now? Don't you think the wires are tapped?"

"And we don't have the slightest bit of dross . . . or of opium."

"Opium? There's some right there," Dondlinger cried out.

They all looked. He was pointing to the little tin left by Auportain on the chest of drawers. Astonishment delayed comprehension. Courvoisier finally picked up the little box, felt its weight in his hands.

"It is; it's opium."

"So Auportain did come while we were at the station!"

"What if it's a trap set by the inspector?"

"But our pipes are still with the cops!"

They talked over the situation. Finally, Marie-Jacqueline went to make more tea, and they all drank a cup laced with the drug. Then, with the police still on their minds and no one willing to go out alone for fear of being followed, they emptied the rest of the precious poison into the toilet. The tin can was thrown into the fire and a strong fragrance of opium spread through the room, coupled with the smell of caramel.

They stayed up until morning, half nodding, half on the lookout, starting from time to time when a sound came from the street or from the staircase. Come daylight, they left one after another, taking roundabout ways to get home. Then, with pointless attempts at cunningness, they set out again in search of their suppliers or their friends to procure the substance that was indispensable to their lives.

It's possible to maintain one's relationships while taking narcotics, but rare are the people for whom this challenge doesn't end in disaster. Dondlinger began by deserting his family. His mother had five children, and the absence of a son was seen as little more than an escape provoked by the whims of his age. He'll come back, they thought . . .

It can be easy for someone from the leisure class, for a business owner or an intellectual, to prolong the compromise between dream and reality, but the effort required to do so is much greater for a blue-collar worker. In Dondlinger's case there was, moreover, an excessively vast difference between his social standing and that of his new friends. He hadn't uprooted from his class: he'd been amputated from it. In one fell swoop he lost his good sense and his clear vision of the world. It was the disequilibrium that opium alone is capable of provoking.

He thus left the company for which he worked based on Courvoisier's promise to find him a better job. Courvoisier employed him for several weeks running errands and paid him when he thought of it or it was convenient.

Dondlinger got used to living in an irregularly paid hotel room, to eating one day in a lavish restaurant and making do the next with a sandwich or a cold piece of boudin washed down with a glass of red wine at the neighborhood café. He was also, during evenings of heightened compassion, the beneficiary of gifts from his friends. He could be seen wearing a tie from Charvey with a cheap, ready-to-wear suit, even shoes from Weston or a chic shoemaker, pants from O'Rossen, a sweater from Prisunic, and cotton socks. His outfit managed nonetheless to provoke envious laughter from his old friends, with the exception, that is, of Bob, who claimed to be an expert in such matters and secretly admired, without really being able to tell the difference between them, the fashion choices of both the pimps at place Blanche and of his Hispano or Rolls-Royce-driving clients.

Though shy with Barbara and her friends, in whose eyes he was truly working class, Dondlinger grew contemptuous toward his friends both from school and from work. He'd forgotten how to speak their language, losing interest in the things that mattered to them and finding himself increasingly bored in their company.

In the end, Courvoisier stopped paying him, and Columot, consequently, offered to take a turn employing him. But Columot was reluctant to bring someone aware of his nighttime activities into the factory.

He consequently came up with tasks whose utility escaped the young man but whose disheartening gratuitousness still managed to have an effect on him.

Moreover, it wasn't long before Columot, more proactive and thus more direct than Courvoisier, let it be known that he wouldn't be able to continue providing for him.

A normal person quickly grows weary of doing favors for a fellow man. The addict even more so. He's indecisive and capricious. Rarely does he keep the numerous promises he makes. A passing cloud, smoke rising from an opium pipe: both carry more weight than his words. It's the only way things can be for someone whose passions are unhindered by any virtue.

So Dondlinger decided to stop using drugs, which he had bought several times but which most often he'd used at the home of one or another of the people who were always willing, or so it seemed at least, to furnish him.

He suffered horribly from the withdrawal. He was addicted and one morning had to beg Antoine for a pellet of opium. It's no good to be poor, and Dondlinger's poverty soon became painfully evident to the others. They found excuses to stop seeing him.

After a night of intolerable suffering, he checked himself into the hôpital Henri-Rousselle.

The morning that Dondlinger went to Henri-Rousselle was veiled in a fog that portended sunshine. The subway was filled with a silent crowd of workers. From the steel viaduct one could look out over the roofs of Paris. He saw in the distance the Church of the Val-de-Grâce, the Panthéon, the Eiffel Tower. Glacière station finally cut off his view.

He walked along a rustic avenue to the consultation ward. The trees quivered in the morning air. Inside a pen, two stags wandered about listlessly near a cement creek and a thatched-roof cabin. They supplemented the visitors' melancholy with cavalier images and affected the behavior of noblemen made blasé through wine, gambling, and women. Tulips adorned the flowerbeds. The hospital was like a charming park, a Port-Royal beyond the reach of the city's sounds.

That evening, Dondlinger was set up in a room furnished with two beds, one of which was already occupied by a poorly shaven individual who treated him like an intruder throughout a two-hour period during which nurses, doctors, and interns stopped by almost every quarter hour. Which didn't prevent the individual from finally exploding into recriminations against the hospital, complaining about having been abandoned and only being treated when the nurses could find the time. He was nearing the end of his treatment and made no effort to conceal his intention of snorting heroin again as soon as he got out.

"Oh, la, la, sir! What a place to be locked away! We're worse off than prisoners here. And this is my third time. They know me quite well by now . . . But I only come when things get really bad. When the cops get too involved and start arresting dealers. That's when I come here. I'm detoxing and they can't do anything to me. But what brutes! They'd watch you die without giving you the tiniest bit of drug. It's an awful place. Getting clean in a week is madness."

But Dondlinger was barely listening to him. He felt protected behind the high walls of Sainte-Anne. He almost wished that he could never leave, that he would be declared mad and end his days in these peaceful surroundings, spending his time carrying out useless little tasks. In the asylums there must be voluntary mental patients, just like there are monks and nuns in the convents and monasteries.

The night passed calmly. The second less so. There was a scramble in the hallway and confabs in hushed voices. Dondlinger clearly heard an intern say:

"Just pretending to make us feel sorry for him. He could have stayed in that position until eight in the morning without dying. Just pretending. They think they can always arouse our sympathy with suicide. But be sure to act like you believe him. If he realizes that we're not idiots, he could try again and succeed."

A young female intern replied:

"They're all actors. I wonder if addiction doesn't actually begin until they've decided to say that they're addicted, when they accept that that's the case and even desire it."

The voices faded down the hallway.

In the morning, Dondlinger found himself alone. His companion had left, cured. But for how long?

He managed the treatment with ease. The frequent shots of Démorphène and stimulants along with the heart and general health examinations filled his days, made the hours go by. He willingly complied, flattered to be looked after by someone, wrongly believing that he was an exceptional case. He prided himself on being a model patient, just as he'd been, several years before, a disciplined soldier. His very docility worried the nurses. So rare is the addict determined to get well, that they interpreted his behavior as deceit and pretense.

"He'll get well, that one," said an intern in the staffroom.

"He'll get well, but he'll start using again because we don't have enough space to keep him here for three months," a veteran said in response. "We get them clean all right, but as soon as they're out they fall back into the world of drugs, into their failing relationships. They again find themselves confronted with their neuroses, with their sexual impotence. They're not ready to face life again. Opium isn't just present in their mental memory, it's in their physical memory as well. And because almost all of them are weak willed, they start using again."

Another intern cited Professor Ball's formula: "You enter morphine addiction through the doors of pain, of hedonism, and of sorrow."

"Yes, that's true, profoundly true; but the expression needs to be revised. Pain, hedonism, sorrow: three different forms of what is more or less the same neurosis. Observe and question our addicts and you'll realize that they all have sexual abnormalities. It ranges from impotence to what could be described as a transposition of love into the domain of dreams. Watch them carefully. In the eyes of the chemist, they all take the same drug. But in reality, one takes it like table wine, the other like brandy or whiskey . . . it's all a matter of temperament. Behind every addiction there's the story of a woman or of the absence of a woman or of disgust for women. That's the case when you're dealing with a man. When you're dealing with a woman . . ."

"It's the same thing except in reverse," said a young man, who was pouring himself something to drink.

"For some you have to advise divorce; others you need to help find a way to be successful in love."

"Basically," said a third, "it's a question of satisfaction. With drugs, they're not only seeking consolation for the pleasure they can't normally experience, but pleasure itself, transposed directly into the brain. It's a kind of unbridled masturbation . . . Pass me the wine, that'll be my conclusion."

"Yes, but as long as we're not able to change our patients' surroundings, our efforts will be for naught. You have to remove them from their family, their friends, their habits. Commit them, if it were possible. But even the asylum's course of treatment wouldn't straighten them out. They all have a great desire for freedom and turn the hate that they unknowingly have for their friends and family against us."

Two days later they gave Dondlinger a new roommate. This one was distraught at not having access to a phonograph, and was simultaneously in love with three American singers: Vaughn de Leath, Sophie Tucker, and Lee Morse. The memory of their voices pursued him, haunted him. He both loved them and hated them for the vigor of their intonation, the tenderness of their voicing. He was jealous from afar of their husbands and their possible lovers.

"Imagine it," he said, "the door opens. A woman comes in. She's beautiful. Her hair falls over her shoulders, her eyes glisten. She comes in and sings 'Some of These Days.' What would you do? Me, I'd hide under my blankets."

But he came brusquely out of his reverie to scream about imaginary forms of treatment. He, as well, accused the doctors of wanting to kill him. He, as well, insisted that the nurses take care of him. He wanted to be tied to an operating table, to receive innumerable injections, to be auscultated and continuously massaged. Dondlinger thought he might go insane listening to him. But still he preferred having him there to the two days of solitude he'd gone through. The physical suffering had diminished. His permanent irritation, brought about by the detoxification, was directed at his noisy roommate instead of the people looking after him.

Then at last he left, freed from his torturer, freed from his poison . . .

As soon as he'd gone through the door, he began thinking about his friends. He felt alone in the city, alone in his life, abandoned, defenseless, weak. Should he go to see Barbara? Columot? Courvoisier? He didn't have a choice in the matter. They alone could save him from the cliff's edge he could feel himself approaching. He needed them: they were more indispensable than the drug and a valuable counterbalance to his family, whom he unknowingly hated.

He walked along beneath the viaduct of the metro while mentally replaying fragments from the past several days, days that now seemed to have lasted a lifetime, to have been as glorious as a legendary battle. He also thought of the imbecile who'd exhausted him with his stories, who'd told him that one time he'd smoked opium with a gas pipe and a piece of a clay pipe, that he'd drank laudanum by the liter, and that nobody, with the exception of himself, was capable of preparing opium in the proper way, with spices and Burgundy. He'd put such a wealth of details into the description of his recipe that the room had seemed to smell like grease in a hotel kitchen and Dondlinger was unable to get the taste of pot roast out of his mouth.

He spat with disgust and went into a bistro to drink his first coffee as a free man.

More than opium, it was love that concerned Antoine, that directed his life and justified his actions. But the one still affected the other. Opium sublimated him at the expense of his desire. He found sentimental satisfactions in the drug that increased the distance between him and his goal, between him and the realization of this desire. He confused Barbara with a ghost that looked like her and which, without realizing it, he preferred to her actual self. He lived inside a misunderstanding and had lost the will to correct it. There was a kind of black magic at work, and although he believed himself to be its sorcerer, he was in fact its object and its dupe.

When he came out of the dream, the dream didn't come out of him. It served as the backdrop to all his actions and brought a layer of fog between him and reality. His vision of Barbara thus colluded with opium to render him powerless. It was only at the price of his very being, of a constant nervous expenditure, that he reacted, that he worked, that he continued down the road that was his destiny.

And he denied all this, denied that it was the most important part of his temperament, and considered only the time spent with Barbara, the actions done to satisfy Barbara, as real life.

When it happened that she needed him to find drugs, he risked his freedom with dangerous adventures that, despite their true banality, excited him.

He consequently developed a fear of the police, of not being able to find what he wanted, of not pleasing her.

Little by little, Antoine's love took a turn. He thought he loved Barbara, but it was himself that he loved through her reflection, it was for himself and to find reasons to love himself that he ran so many risks.

At certain moments, he was aware of how he actually felt. But he would then force these revelations from his mind. It would be death's responsibility to one day set him down face to face with himself and make him realize that Barbara and her ghost were only concealing his own image in an imaginary mirror.

Now that he was out of the hospital, Dondlinger felt suddenly alone in the world. His family seemed stupid, tactless, irritating. His job disgusted him. His former friends had lost track of him, forgotten him. They'd met new people.

He would think of Barbara's group with bitterness. Courvoisier, Columot—both had disappointed him. Neither one had kept his promises. He didn't dare go back to see Barbara. He was poorer than ever and found himself isolated at the very moment he most needed the warmth of friendship.

Then one afternoon he ran into Antoine. He latched onto him, confided his desperation and the most secret stirrings of his soul. Moved, Antoine took him home and, naturally, proposed that they smoke so as to find some solace. Perhaps Antoine was thinking of his old jealousy and, without admitting it to himself, was happy to see a rival out of the race.

They conversed with the typical effusion brought about by opium. Things had happened during Dondlinger's absence. While listening to news of the group, Dondlinger found himself overcome by nostalgia and the pain of exclusion became stronger still.

They ate together that evening. At the end of the meal, Antoine, who was planning to go to Barbara's, couldn't decide whether or not to bring along his guest. He was unable, however, to withstand the distress he saw in Dondlinger's expression when he said that he should be going.

"You ought to come along. I'm going to Barbara's. I'm sure she'll be happy to see you."

Dondlinger was too weak to say no. Barbara delightfully welcomed him back. He was a novelty, a traveler returning from some distant place. They asked him at length about the treatment at Henri-Rousselle, and no one was surprised to see him accept a pipe.

They saw him again the following day, and in the days that followed that. Less than a week later he was addicted again, and by that point he'd lost the ephemeral interest bestowed upon him by his time at the hospital. He was once again the intruder, the scrounger, the borrower of drugs never paid for. But he needed opium so badly that he put up with every affront. He was irrevocably enslaved.

Columot hung up his telephone so furiously that he broke the earpiece. He stood up, paced about his office, and called for his secretary. He began to dictate a letter: "My dear friend, I have an urgent need to speak with you regarding Dunois, the stockbroker. I've tried in vain to reach you by telephone . . ." He stopped.

"Tear that up. I'm going out. I'll be back this afternoon."

He went down into the courtyard where workers were unloading a truck, got into his car, and started off. He sped toward the center of Paris, made a sharp turn on place des Victoires, and, following rue Vide-Gousset, came to a stop in front of Notre-Dame des Victoires. He went into the church. The darkness shrouded him in its domino cloak. The decor brought to mind Italian festivals, gentlemanly conversations, and, also, a worldly austerity. The slabs on the floor seemed to have been worn away by tears. So long had this place been a sanctuary of pain and hope that it was impossible for the air not to be permeated with these two emotions. It was a crossroads for sorrows of the heart. Mothers came to ask for the lives of their sons, prostitutes for freedom from their pimps. In addition to the Catholic atmosphere, something pagan—a spirit from before the age of Christianity, from even further back than the time when a temple dedicated to Venus had likely stood here—ran through the nave of this place, which since prehistory had been predestined to great effusions of the heart, the senses, the imagination.

Like a regular, Columot went to the back of the church, bought a candle from the little stand set up on the left, and, after crossing the nave, lit and set it before the altar of the chapel, which was covered with ex-voto and scented by the melting wax of countless, already burning candles.

He went into a corner and said: "As you can see, it's me. I've come back to find you. I can't promise you anything. I don't have anything to tell you about myself. I'm still an unbeliever, but I trust you. You know why I've come, so there's no point in saying it. I'm unhappy. I'm in danger. Help me. Consider my initiative in coming here. I don't know what's brought me to your church. Maybe it's you. Maybe you have a plan for me. I don't know where you're leading me. But as you can see, I've let myself be led here. Please, help me, protect me."

As if afraid of being recognized, he went out through a little door that led to the sacristy and looked out over the courtyard of the second arrondissement's district council. Following rue de la Banque, he went back to the front of Notre-Dame des Victoires for his car. Then, reassured, smiling for what was to come, he drove leisurely toward the Champs-Élysées in search of a friend to have a drink with before lunchtime and the afternoon, the latter of which was reserved for financial matters.

Arichetti's specter tormented Antoine, Barbara, Columot, Courvoisier. More sensitive in certain ways than their other friends, they saw in him a dark portent of the future they were preparing for themselves, a grave-riddled future, waiting for the time when their own would come to take its place in the line of a funereal aisle where, they knew, memories would bring few people and, what was more certain, evoke little curiosity from others. They prevented themselves from thinking about it by sinking further still into daily intoxication.

As sensitive as they were, but by nature more pessimistic, Auportain had, by all appearances, scratched Arichetti from his memory. But, though no one would have guessed that Arichetti was still on his mind, it was Auportain of all people who suggested to Barbara that they go visit him. Maybe—and who would have thought otherwise?—he was hoping it would help turn the young woman away from a lifestyle he regularly criticized for its false tragedy, its illusory grandeur, its mediocrity.

Columot, who had a morbid interest in the horrific, drove them in his powerful car. This robust young man, full of life and a potential model of stability, hid an anxiety that he thought drugs helped to extinguish but which they in fact maintained and fortified.

The event was as terrifying as both Auportain, as a way to frighten them, and Columot, as a way to satisfy his appetite for the lurid, could have hoped it would be. When they left Arichetti, who'd been unable to recognize them and had sunken to a place beyond any possible hope of recovery, Columot thought back on the perilous days of 1917, when he'd been fully aware of the great fortune that was life. He remembered in detail this or that sunny day, during the course of which he'd brushed against death so many times that he'd concluded it was powerless against him. He could again see the crazed face of a German pilot whose aircraft, shot down by Columot himself, had grazed his own, tearing off an aileron as it passed. He could again feel the weight of his eyelids when he'd closed them the moment after he'd landed his crippled plane. The echo of his comrades' voices as they'd rushed up to free his unscathed body from the pile of scrap and plywood resonated through the years. He saw the twisted smile on his engineer's face. His memory of the whiskey he'd drunk afterward at the bar made him salivate.

"How can they treat someone like that?" said Barbara. "These crazy houses are prisons! The people who run them are barbaric."

"No," said Auportain. "Just over a century ago you would have found Arichetti in chains. Yes, it's true that he might not have gone crazy, since back then they didn't have cocaine, heroin, or even, really, opium. People don't appreciate the progress made by Pinel, who taught us to treat the insane as if they were suffering from an illness. We've made huge leaps in recent years. And we'll make many more yet. Maybe we'll even succeed in curing insanity. But medicine is always struggling against legislation. In Arichetti's case, it's less his actual insanity that's the cause of the condition we saw him in than the consequences of his insanity, his senility. But what can you say about the laws concerning addicts? You're viewed as being guilty of something. I'm not speaking of myself: I'm completely responsible, completely guilty, and I don't deserve to be in prison simply because in France suicide isn't a crime. But you? Guilty of something? No, you're victims. It's not the dealers that create smokers, snorters, and injectors. It's the other way around. I salute the Pinels of the future who will strike down the current prejudices and allow you to be healed. This will happen when we know how to heal injured feelings, thwarted intelligence, weakened willpower. In reality, it's the entire social system that needs changing, because it's the social system that's responsible for your existence, it's the aggravation of the social system's illness that leads to the recruitment of your unfortunate kind. But I'm talking too much. Let's leave money with the bursar for that miserable soul and sink back into our reflections and our sorrows. If only this visit could free you . . . from where you are now . . . from where you're going."

Outside life went on as usual, but all three, in different ways, felt excluded from it. They were painfully conscious of the city's restlessness. The very motions and obligations of life irritated them and often seemed insurmountable. Auportain had removed them by meticulously organizing his existence. Barbara's large fortune protected her from them. As for Columot, he was afflicted not only by every last one of their demands, but also by those of his business, a particularly frenzied form of work. He, more than the others, missed his youth. He, more precisely than the others, was aware of their self-imposed downfall and degradation. But he admired Auportain all the more for having experienced life before choosing to drop out of it, for not talking about his problems, for being a partner to rather than a slave of opium. Was this admirable, in the end? He suddenly asked himself the question. Hadn't old Uncle

Columot, who'd lived for his store and for his family, gone down the right path as well? It was true that things ended tragically for him. But what was the point of thinking about it? Three pipes in the evening and all of this would vanish in that wonderful fragrance.

Auportain wasn't the kind of man who could tolerate a depressing atmosphere for very long. He parted ways with Barbara and Columot as soon as they reached Paris.

The evening was still a long way off. Columot drove along the outlying boulevards through scenes filled with factories, empty lots, and railway bridges. After having wandered through neighborhoods whose miserable vastness matched their interior nightmare, he stopped the car along the Saint-Martin canal.

Children watched the lock being operated. Several people out on a stroll contemplated the brown water, which reflected the barges.

"Columot," said Barbara, "if we're going to end up like Arichetti, we might as well get it over with now. All you need to do is press on the gas and go straight into the canal."

"That water's rather dirty," said Columot with a sigh, whose morose train of thought had been interrupted by Barbara's proposition. "And, besides, there's nothing original or romantic about drowning yourself in a canal. I'd never kill myself. I always hope that tomorrow will be better than today."

"Do you believe in God?"

"Me? Not at all. It's not even a question I've considered. I've never been a believer, and that's enough to make me say that I'll never be one. Actually, the more I think about it, the less I need his presence. The universe seems mysterious enough as it is, and God wouldn't add anything to it, wouldn't explain anything. Live? Why? Because, quite simply, that's how things are. Since I'm guaranteed to die, one day I'll know what life and death are, if they're anything at all. But to live? I'll take every bit of life that's allotted to me even if it's not always easy to swallow. You never know. Strange things could happen one day."

"I believe in God."

"Then you shouldn't be thinking about killing yourself. Religion forbids it."

"Oh, religion's not God. I'm sure he'd forgive me if I committed suicide. He might think I'm foolish, but he wouldn't see me as wicked. What good do I serve anyway?"

"There's nothing to suggest that our purpose is to be useful."

"But you're useful, Columot. You do something. You live. I even wonder how you can smoke and work. But me . . . I sometimes go weeks without knowing what color the sky is, or even what season it is. The theater from time to time, bars, a dinner with boring people who still manage to have a good time."

"It's up to no one but yourself to change all that. Get clean."

"Get clean yourself."

"I'm considering it, Barbara, and more seriously than you might think."

Bells rang out in the distance. A light breeze blew over the canal. Birds chirped in a tree. The glass door of a café closed loudly after several energetic young men had come through it, sailors headed back to their barge.

The car moved slowly along the embankment.

They encountered a crowd again near the Square du Temple and place de la République. They avoided the bigger streets by following a circuitous route through the smaller ones, astonishingly gray, astonishingly dreary, behind the facades of which one could sense the efforts of numberless men and women working joyless jobs. Most of them were thinking ahead to next Sunday—and it would be a festive, springtime Sunday—to the next vacation, and these vacations, as mediocre as they were, would be scented with wild flowers and cool rivers.

They came to the newer neighborhoods, straight as a die, swept, clean, without shops, without life, without cheer. They'd passed the work sites, the factories, and the workshops. They were now coming to the false garden of the rich neighborhoods, the soulless cemetery of Paris.

Columot dropped Barbara off and went back to his office. His financial situation was becoming a concern for him. However much energy he might have had, he was still subjected to the demands of opium. Under its influence he neglected numerous obligations and ceaselessly put off until the next day the ones whose tedium he couldn't face. As he'd said, he had a blind confidence in the future, putting his faith in it as if it were a talisman capable of instantly dissolving all perils, of removing all obstacles.

But that day, more than usual, his work seemed to be dreadfully futile, and he made do with hastily delivered updates from a departmental head and a secretary. He was then about to go begin an evening indistinguishable from so many others that had made up the past weeks and years.

But before he could leave, an employee stopped him and handed over two personally addressed letters. The names of two suppliers were written on the envelopes. Their sight caused him to feel a deep unease, and he was shocked to find himself shaking as he opened them.

His distress passed quickly. He grew once again calm when the content of the letters brought him face to face with an imminent catastrophe, a catastrophe he'd been anticipating but which drugs had pushed into the future, while he'd been placing all his hope on some impossible miracle.

Columot spent the next two days and nights with accountants, bankers, suppliers, clients, which is to say, with debtors and creditors. He relied on heroin, taking doses almost twice as large as he was accustomed to.

After those two days, the situation was clear. He'd reached agreements that would save him if he could simultaneously monitor his own activity and that of his partners. Indeed, he was right in fearing that, at the first sign of collapse, they would try to rob him of the profits he'd generated. But he felt shattered by fatigue and drug use. He understood that he was going to collapse just before reaching the finish line. He sent a telegram to his uncle Mazurier, his mother's brother, who lived in Angoulême and whom he hadn't seen for years.

Life is mediocre for the one who surrenders to opium. An idler, he lives only through the drug and for the drug, and little by little he abandons the usual gestures by which a man manifests his existence. And this very idleness adds a new danger to that of the drug. A woman forsakes the basic maintenance of her beauty, even of her decency. A man slowly loses any memory of how he'd once been. They move from dream to sleep, and from sleep to the demands of their addiction. At this point smoking or snorting isn't needed only by the mind, it's needed, and even more so, by the body. And it's this physical desire that ends up erasing any trace of joy, of elation.

Should the smoker want to go on exercising any other activity, the conflict between work, ambition, and the illusory satisfaction brought about by nights filled with hollow dreams worsens.

Antoine knew this struggle well, knew how much energy was needed to move from the couch, upon which he'd traveled through the darkness, into the glaring light of day. His work had preserved him, protected him. On certain evenings, he preferred good old natural sleep to gilded insomnia, and would go to bed without seeing anyone, without going to any gatherings. This didn't surprise his friends. The addict often misses get-togethers, often breaks promises.

One evening Antoine got a call from Barbara. Feverishly, she asked him to find whatever he could for the night, even if it was laudanum or Paregoric—the final recourse in case of shortage. Antoine was tired, he didn't have much money, and he was in the grip of a melancholy brought about by the awareness of the vertiginous chasm he was approaching.

However, with an enthusiasm provoked by his anxiety, his sadness, and his boredom, he went out in a desperate search for the drugs Barbara needed. He endured humiliating refusals from his friends, suspicion from dealers who had never met him, fear of being watched. At last he found several precious grams of opium and called Barbara to tell her he was coming over. She replied in a weak but elated voice. A taxi drove him quickly over to her place. But when he arrived, she wasn't there. A note pinned to the door informed him that she couldn't wait and had gone to a friend's. A powerful anger came over Antoine.

"Ah!" he said loudly, "I hope she dies!"

This wasn't a wish uttered simply out of disappointment, for at that instant, with his entire body, with his entire soul, with all the energy contained within his sexual desires and his feelings of love, he truly wished that Barbara would die. The word "death" filled his heart and brain, and not only the word but the thing itself, with all the accompanying tears and regrets, the decomposition. He imagined the details of Barbara's death, the maggots eating away at her beautiful body. For a moment, he was Barbara herself, dying in a landscape filled with clouds and rocks, he was her pain and regrets, her anxiety and anguish. Perhaps Antoine had never loved Barbara more than at this very moment, as he was writing out her destiny with the concentration worthy of a spell. He merged with her in a lover's embrace, but it was a love that had incorporated the purest and most powerful form of hatred. It was impossible for such a feeling not to cross over into the material world, and Antoine immediately feared the realization of his wish. But his fear resembled hope. What if on this very evening he was on the verge of ruination, and it could only be prevented by the death of his closest, clearest, most beloved adversary? Barbara! The name rang out like a bell and suddenly, since he was out on the street, engrossed in the furious struggle taking place in his mind, he heard a real bell ring out. It was coming from a school. The sound was reedy and caused him to envision a desolate landscape, a cemetery that had been abandoned for thousands and thousands of years and with indecipherable epitaphs written on the tombstones, tombstones which weren't scattered among grass but in the depths of the earth, already waiting for the work of archaeologists. Antoine wasn't himself. He was Barbara or, rather, Barbara's corpse, and even Barbara's ghost, and heavy metaphysical sobs smothered the words he was saying to himself. The city was sleeping. He walked on. Dawn found him at the edge of the Seine, beyond Saint-Cloud. Bargemen had just pulled a drowned body out of the water. He approached, convinced that it was Barbara's. But no—it was a large woman bloated with fat and water. The only articles of clothing that could still be distinguished were a blue canvas apron and a pair of horribly warped shoes. Her face showed such pain, such wounded tenderness, that the young man felt tears come to his eyes. He imagined the years of toil this person, who'd once been a young girl, a young woman, a lover, a mother, had endured. Somber domestic tragedies played out in his mind. Water ran down from the body's clothing, the swollen stomach throbbed. Antoine went back up the stone stairs that had brought him down to the water.

And, ceaselessly, he repeated to himself: "I hope she dies! I hope she dies!"

His wish occupied the entirety of his mind, directed every last one of his thoughts. He pictured his beloved's final moments, savoring the horrible scene. Like a vulture exploring a decaying piece of carrion, he sunk his head into the stomach that had been refused him, into the brain that hadn't spent enough time thinking about him. But there were birds singing in the trees, and the sun was rising above the rooftops. And Antoine was nothing more than a machine walking through the streets and avenues. He found the Bois de Boulogne and took refuge there, like a hunted animal. He walked from the lawns of Bagatelle to the Palmarium, which in his trance he renamed Columbarium, the symbol of utter and irrevocable death. He came to the Longchamp and Auteuil racecourses. The woods were empty. Suddenly, along a bridleway, a hunchback wearing a light-colored suit passed by on a horse. The woods were coming to life. He got into a passing taxi and fell into a deep sleep, and the driver had to wake him when they arrived at his building. He staggered up the stairs to his room. He sank swiftly into sleep, overcome with sorrow and horror at having confronted his own thoughts.

The shadows of four heads were cast onto the ceiling, four heads gathered around a small oil lamp. Sometimes a slight flash shone from a skillfully maneuvered metal needle. On the porcelain bowl, the resinous opium settled with a crackle. The smoker inhaled, then the expelled smoke dispersed throughout the room. The doorbell rang. Courvoisier went to answer.

"Who is it?" shouted Barbara from the couch.

"It's Dondlinger."

"Ah, damn! Him again," she murmured. (Then louder:) "Let him in!—You've come at a bad time," she said to him, "we're talking about business and we're almost out of drugs. All I can offer you is a bit of dross in a cup of tea."

The words made Dondlinger freeze. Courvoisier had lain back down. The two others, Berthe and a man he didn't know, neither moved nor spoke. He sat down in the darkness. A long moment went by. Barbara said:

"You'll find the tea in the kitchen and the dross on the fireplace. Help yourself, don't bother me, don't make any noise, don't talk to me."

Obediently, he went to boil water before making himself a cup of tea that was as black as coffee. He dissolved the opium in it and, since he didn't know where the sugar was, swallowed the tea as it was. It filled his mouth with a strong bitterness that dried his throat and matched his current state of mind. He wasn't sure if he wanted to go back into the smoking room. Finally, he made up his mind and, with very soft steps, went to the entryway. Through the half-opened door he could hear Barbara's voice.

"I'm going to go away for two or three months. I'm too high-strung. And it's irritating not being able to see who you want, and only who you want."

Dondlinger didn't immediately establish a link between this sentence and himself, but it bothered him all the same and engraved itself onto his memory. The subway had stopped running. He had only one desire: to lie on a set of cushions until morning and be forgotten by the others.

Then a sudden realization only served to make the situation more painful. The stranger had lifted himself up onto his elbow, the lamp was now illuminating his face, and Dondlinger recognized Columot. So, the man in whom he'd confided one morning, to whom he'd opened up his heart, who'd called himself his friend and whom he'd believed to be his friend, hadn't even said good evening. He knew now that he was an intruder, an outsider, in this circle to which he'd so desperately hoped to belong. The barriers of wealth separating him from the others hadn't been knocked down. Or, possibly, they'd been rebuilt. They'd sent him to the pantry like a servant they wanted out of the way, and he alone was the cause of this disconcerting silence. More than anything else, he felt distant from Barbara. Her kisses had simply been a passing fancy, a whim, a bit of fun. These other men had so much more to offer than he did. Take lighthearted and fine-talking Courvoisier, for instance, so funny, so unpredictable; and then Columot, of course, who radiated strength, security, the virility of a man who gave in to amorous adventures and the challenges of life. He was undoubtedly a nuisance, and the scene before his eyes was intolerable.

"Barbara," he said, "if you don't mind I'll go into the bathroom to lie down on some cushions to nod comfortably."

"Mister Dondlinger will do as he wishes. Mister Dondlinger, love of my life, little monkey of my menagerie, is at home here," Barbara responded.

Dondlinger assured himself that this was just a joke.

He settled into the bathroom, determined to forget his feelings of discomfort. But then, on a pipe, he noticed the solder that he himself had made on his first visit to the apartment, and an inner fire spread through his body. He decided to explain himself. He got up and went toward the living room. He could soon hear Barbara talking.

"But, Columot, why shouldn't I call him my monkey? He *is* my monkey, after all, and nothing else. He can be amusing, but I've had enough fun with him. I'll find a way to make sure he doesn't come back. This is enough. My God, he thinks he can get away with whatever he wants, which I wouldn't tolerate from anyone. I'm done excusing his bad upbringing. There's no reason I should let myself be taken advantage of even more than I already have."

There was no one else they could have been talking about. For a moment, he wanted to go in and explode with anger. But he held himself back. He decided to save this confrontation for another day and, taking refuge in the bathroom, waited for the light of dawn to begin whitening the window. When it did, he got up to leave.

Before going out, he looked into the living room. Barbara was asleep in Columot's arms. Berthe was on another couch. Courvoisier was laid out next to a heater. The memory of the morning spent with Columot opened inside him like an old wound. He left, and was surprised and overwhelmed by the bustle out on the street. He'd slept for longer than he'd realized. It was already almost eleven o'clock. He felt extremely tired.

Dondlinger counted his money. Sixty francs. He walked aimlessly for a while, then, suddenly, climbed onto the bus for the Saint-Lazare train station. He found a seat at the Critérion and drank, slowly, a jug of stout. He was half dreaming. The world seemed to be made of cotton. From time to time, Barbara's words replayed in his mind:

"He *is* my monkey, after all . . ."

Ah, he was her monkey! Well, we'll see about that. This monkey was going to make her cry . . . and he imagined Barbara, years later, one evening at twilight, thinking of him and being touched by the memory.

"He was so nice. But I wasn't always so nice with him. He loved me and I must have hurt him, time and time again."

He was experiencing Barbara's future compassion himself, for himself. A wave of sadness rushed through his mind. He remembered when, as a child, he'd gone on an excursion train to spend the day in Dieppe. They'd played, he and the other children, on the city's pebble-covered beach. They threw the stones into the water, some of which skipped between the waves. He could again smell the scent of sand and wet stones. Beneath his feet, dry algae cracked into pieces. But no, he was here, in his poorly cut, worn-out suit, having a drink in an expensive café like a dandy. He might as well enjoy himself. He ordered a whiskey, the taste of which brought to mind evenings spent at Barbara's, or at his other friends' apartments. What will they say, when will they find out? They'll of course have regrets, maybe they'll even feel remorse. "He was a nice guy, that Dondlinger, even if he wasn't from our world. And it wasn't him who came knocking at our door. It was Barbara that found him, snatched him from his work, his life, his future. Without her, he would have found himself a serious young woman. They would have lived happily together." Calm Sundays at La Garenne, or at the stadium to watch a soccer game, and then little dinners in a quiet bistro, a little car . . . I'm an idiot to be thinking about them, about Barbara who doesn't give a damn about me. All the same, she's so lovely, Barbara, so beautiful! Her monkey!

He got up, went into the station, and bought a ticket for Le Pecq. How fast the train went! And how pleasant was the journey. The passing landscapes were as pretty as pictures; one's eye was drawn to the happy-looking houses, the quiet little gardens, and sometimes further out toward the horizon, which was soon filled with tall trees.

The station at Le Pecq was empty. He consulted an employee. The train from Paris would soon be arriving. He went across the tracks and waited on the platform, with a slight pain at his temples and a buzzing in his ears that made him dizzy. In the well-trimmed bushes a bird hopped about. Suddenly, the train appeared. Dondlinger settled his foot firmly against the edge of the platform, put his hands behind his back in the same way he had, years before, when he went roller skating and tried to imitate the great champions. The train was approaching. With all his strength, he threw himself into it, head first. His skull split open. Brain came spurting out. The bird flew off. The engineer, pale, swore and braked sharply.

Heads appeared at the doors. The ticket inspector on the platform gestured with large movements to the station master. He couldn't speak: he felt like vomiting.

Estival was daydreaming with a sheet of paper set in front of him. Where would he spend his vacation? The sea? The mountains? The door opened and a colleague entered to join him in his idling.

"So Estival, how's business?"

"The job? Shit in a bottle. Still dealing with addicts. Don't touch this, don't touch that, filling out forms, bothering people. You get welcomed like a beggar by people who talk down to you. You arrest people who don't have the right connections. And then . . . half of them walk free. I spent a week at the public prosecutor's just to swipe a file that I sent too early and desperately needed back."

"What do you expect? Nothing you say will change anything. All you can do is do your job, and not try to understand or improve the world. This will all last as long as we do."

"Even so, it's all so idiotic. I know all these people by now. And they know me, too. They're not hoodlums. They're just wretches. We throw them in prison, some of them, sometimes, when the bosses get worked up. Then they get out and start using again. It'd be better if we put them into treatment."

"Treatment? You sound like a child. You know full well that they're incurable. They're chronic users. We'd have to lock them up for the rest of their life. And don't forget, there're others besides the addicts. You have the dealers, too, who're nothing more than crooks."

"Crooks, yes. But they'll always be around. If they weren't doing this, they'd be doing something else. Maybe they'd beat up little old ladies or rob cars. Anyway, crooks or not, they're also protected. It's not the dealers who create the addicts. It's the other way around. It'd be better to register the users and give them their drugs through the state. It'd be safer, anyway. And besides, we know all the drug dealers. We work with them for God's sake. They're the ones who give us all our information. The big ones don't risk anything. They pull in millions. The smaller ones, they're . . . the ones we arrest when they stop playing by the rules and force us to take action against them. We don't fix anything. You could even say we make things worse. Listen, old pal. Three years ago heroin showed up on rue de Lappe. All the smalltime gangsters in the neighborhood stuffed it up their nostrils. Cocaine, that's over. It's old hat. It was popular before 1914, and even during the war. But no one's been using it since 1920."

"Well, cocaine, heroin, opium: it's all the same."

"Sure, of course. But about a month ago I found heroin at the home of a blue-collar worker. You get what I'm saying? Workers, decent, honest people. Not pimps dressed up as workers. In twenty years, the whole world will be taking it. Not just whores and the rich, but the people. And we'll go on with our nonsense, writing up files based on information from informants, arresting the unfortunate ones, and that will be that."

"And we'll get paid at the end of the month. That's enough. You don't make the laws. You apply them, period. Anyway, come play a game of belote and get your mind off of all this. If you look at everything under a microscope you turn either senile or become an anarchist."

"It's just all so idiotic!"

"I don't understand why you get so worked up about these people. They're worthless."

"But they're not worthless. There are some splendid men among them . . . and women! Listen, I know a scientist, a physicist . . . he'll end up behind bars and that will be that. It would be idiotic and cruel to lock them up. But it would be more honest than playing cat-and-mouse with them, and setting traps for them! This isn't a man's job they're making us do, no, they're turning us into blackmailers!"

One of the smokers lifted the curtain. He saw, in the east, a pale light announcing the arrival of morning.

"It's dawn," he said.

"Already?" Simonne said with surprise. "I've got to get going. My husband's bringing my daughters over soon. As we speak, they're on a train somewhere near Lyon. What would they think if they didn't find me at home? They don't know anything about my little escapades."

She was a woman of forty, always cheerful, still youthful, who rarely came to the smoking sessions. She had to either be on her own or be able to get away from her family for a few hours in the afternoon. After twenty years of marriage, her husband treated her more like a business partner than a spouse. The exhaustion of childrearing, the monotony of their jobs, and even idleness itself had little by little opened up a gulf in their marriage. Opium was a refuge, a secret pleasure she allowed herself from time to time. And she loved the company of these entertaining, whimsical outsiders.

She quickly got dressed and left. They heard a taxi brake out in the street. A door slammed shut and then the engine grew louder.

"Where the hell, Barbara, did you find her?"

"She's a childhood friend. She knew me when I was little and we'd play together. Two or three years ago, she was feeling down and told me how bored she was; so I proposed that we smoke . . . It's good for her. Conjugal life isn't always fun. Her husband's friends are dull, and she likes to have a good time. You should have seen her ten years ago . . . she was one of the prettiest women in Paris."

"Does she smoke at home?"

"What do you think? She's petrified someone will notice the smell, and she's so afraid her husband will catch her that she doesn't even do heroin."

"But she was there that day we all went to the station with Courvoisier."

"Her husband wasn't home. She's a funny woman. A combination of prudence and audacity."

"And yet despite all that she sniffed quite a dose of powder before leaving. When her dignified husband gets back she'll surely be high."

"Bah! She'll say she's sick."

Simonne meanwhile had arrived back home. The elevator took her up to the building's top floor, where she lived in an immense apartment. She took the key from her purse and tried to put it into the lock. She couldn't.

"I took too much," she thought. "I'm feeling a little dizzy now."

The light, on a time switch, went out. She looked for the button but couldn't find it. Through the window on the landing, the light of dawn was slowly seeping in.

She decided to sit down and wait for daybreak. She didn't want to ring, wake up a maid, make her be privy to her late arrival.

She stood back up and tried again to open the door.

Suddenly, she felt as heavy as lead. A bright light dazzled her, burnt her eyelids.

"Another dizzy spell . . ." she said weakly.

These were her last words. She fell like a sledgehammer. Her husband and daughters tried to lift up her already cold body when they got home from the train station.

Arichetti's mother was a simple-minded little woman, curt, suspicious, and voluble. She showed up at Barbara's apartment one afternoon, without warning. The building had intimidated her, and she expected to be shown by a maid, after a long wait, into a drape-filled living room where she'd find a noble lady wearing a ceremonial dress. She almost lost her composure when Barbara herself opened the door, disheveled and in a bathrobe, and told the woman that she was Barbara Durand. As for Barbara, she assumed the other woman was a drug dealer and almost slammed the door in her face. But, hastily, the woman said that she was Arichetti's mother, Mme Arichetti, and that she'd come to thank her for looking after her unfortunate son.

Facing one another in the living room, they could come up with nothing to talk about. Mechanically, Barbara poured herself a large glass of brandy and offered one to her visitor. She stiffly refused. Because she'd come with a specific goal in mind. If Barbara had given money to the asylum it meant that she was her son's mistress and that he, no doubt, had gone crazy because of her. The damages had to be covered.

"My son," she said curtly, "is a handsome, intelligent, hard-working boy. He had his whole future in front of him. When he gets better he'll make himself a lot of money. He'll be a sought-after bachelor and make the girl he marries very happy. Serious as he is . . . and orderly," she added while looking around the room. "He's not a womanizer, not a drinker, not a gambler . . . nothing done to excess. I hope he'll marry a woman he loves and who loves him in return."

As she said these words, she looked into Barbara's astounded eyes with a sharp expression. Barbara almost chocked on her brandy, torn as she was between indignation, a desire to laugh, and a desire to cry. She stood up.

"So whom does he love?" she asked.

"You ought to know better than I do. It's a matter for the heart and the conscience. Marie-Louis . . ." (and the sound of this first name, so rarely used by Arichetti's friends, resonated bizarrely in Barbara's ears, had the effect of an uninvited guest's arrival). "Marie-Louis is a model son. Right up until the day he fell ill, he was helping me with things. Because he loves his mother. Oh, I raised him well. I deprived myself of everything to make sure he turned out the way he did. And it's terribly difficult to see so much effort go to waste! An asylum for the insane!"

Her voice faltered on these final words, as if they were some shameful confession, and she forced back either a sob or a pang of nausea.

It was difficult to tell which emotion she was succumbing to: greed, pride, or a distressed maternal love. The three sentiments were no doubt competing inside her little brain, and although capable of loving zealously and equally her son, a mediocre respectability, and money, she was certainly a stranger to any form of higher-level thinking.

Barbara tried to picture the coupling that could have begot such a son from such a mother. The only images that came to mind were scenes of rape during an evening battle or orgies in the darkness of a ruined house.

"What about his father?" she said.

"His father? He never told you that we were abandoned before he was born? There's no point in wondering where he is now. What good could come out of it? Besides, they don't even look alike."

Barbara wondered which of his ancestors Arichetti was indebted to for his finesse, his unaffected grace, his insouciance, his imagination.

"So, mademoiselle," the stubborn old lady went on, "what are you going to do?"

Barbara was tired, tired of listening to her, tired of thinking about Arichetti. She took a bundle of thousand-franc notes from a drawer.

"Here . . . take this . . . to help him . . . and yourself. But leave immediately."

Carefully, the old woman counted the money.

"There's thirty-five thousand francs here. Do you want a receipt?"

"No . . . goodbye now."

She showed her out and closed the door. Suddenly, she reopened it.

"And don't come back. Never come back. Anyway, I'm leaving Paris. I'm going to America. Farewell."

Her shoulders rounded, her lips pinched tightly together, Mademoiselle Arichetti went down the stairs, holding the purse with the thirty-five thousand francs inside it against her heart.

Courvoisier arrived late to Lily's. Her room smelt like must and she was still in bed. Courvoisier took her into his arms, but the smell of her body and the bed repulsed him. She had something to drink brought up from a neighboring café. She spoke breathlessly, and with an animation that brought an unhealthy shade of red to her cheeks. Sometimes her mouth went dry and she would take a sip of her drink before continuing with her speech.

"I asked Barbara for money. Would you believe that she refused to lend me any? She's already given me enough, she said. I'd like to ask you for a little. When I had money, I didn't even give it a second thought. I never said no to my friends. I gave away jewels, dresses, without even mentioning drugs! Barbara would come over here. My little Lily this, my little Lily that. But we'll see who has the last laugh. Don't think that I'm going to spend my whole life here. I'm going to spend the winter resting. In the spring I'll get clean and be finished with drugs. I'm an attractive girl and there's no shortage of men who'd be only too happy to love me. I've lived too much for other people. I've wasted too much time helping this or that person. What has it gotten me? I'm asking you . . . to think that some stuck-up girl refuses to lend me two thousand francs. She owes me more that in drugs! And the risks I took buying them for her . . ."

She got up. Courvoisier saw that she'd been going to bed in her slip and, furthermore, that she was dirty. Her neglected hair showed traces of an old Auburn dye that he remembered had been a birthday present from Barbara.

Lily began to apply nail polish while she went on talking. Then she put on a coral necklace. Another gift from Barbara. On the table a comb bristling with tufts of hair sat next to a petit-suisse and a stale piece of bread. She put on a lady's suit that Courvoisier could remember having seen on Barbara. Likewise the dust-covered evening dress hanging from a coat rack.

"Why don't we go and get a drink? Take me to the Chatham, like you used to."

"Not tonight, I don't have time. We can go somewhere nearby if you want."

Lily smiled sadly.

"You're ashamed of me, too."

She took the familiar little rectangle of white paper from her purse, along with a nail file. In front of the mirror, she snorted a dose of heroin.

"Thank God I've got heroin . . . I'd kill myself without it." (Then suddenly:) "My sweet Courvoisier, help me out. Let me borrow thirty francs so I can buy a gram."

"I can't. I only have fifty on me. I can give you twenty if you want. I'll make change at the bistro."

"Listen, let's not go and give me thirty, I'm begging you. It'll come out to the same thing. You'd surely end up spending ten francs on the aperitif."

Courvoisier went down to get change. He came back up and gave her the money.

"You're a good guy. I'll be okay for a couple of days now. Thank you."

Courvoisier was overcome by a profound sadness. The image reflected in the mirror was cruel. He could, on his own face, see the signs of decline that would eventually lead him to the same point as Lily.

He went slowly down the narrow stairwell and its threadbare carpet. It was almost dusk. He went out, alone, into the streets of Paris. At an intersection he saw Antoine Maison, who passed by without noticing him. Or maybe he was intentionally avoiding him. He shrugged, not knowing if this gesture of contempt was meant for his friend or for himself.

As for Lily, her memory was already fading away into the fog that also concealed his future. It would be a bad idea to see her again. He didn't want to, and fate would see to it that their paths didn't cross again. Where did she finally vanish to? On what beach of life did this piece of human wreckage wash up on to die? It was no longer his responsibility to worry about it. One evening or another he would find himself thinking about her again. Sometimes she was a dazzling Lily on a festive evening, laughing brightly with a drink in hand. And sometimes, in the warm glow of a smoking session, he saw her attractive face lit up by the opium lamp, her expression growing serious as she inhaled from the pipe. But, more often, he had a vision of a fallen woman without charm, grace, or decency, whose name, now more or less forgotten, had once been tenderly pronounced by smiling lips.

Marie-Jacqueline had been living at Lily's for several weeks when Berthe died of peritonitis brought on by a pellet of opium. Several days later, Jeanne, in turn, succumbed to a bout of typhoid fever.

The two young women, deep down, felt no particular sorrow or emotion. From these two deaths, which Noëlle had come over to tell them about, they took little more than a bit of sustenance for sentimental discussions. And they would never see Noëlle again, either. What happened to her, no one ever found out. They simply stopped seeing her. Such disappearances occur frequently in the world of opium. The missing are spoken of for a little while longer than in other circles, but one expects to see them again the next day, or even years later, through some chance encounter. Had she died, gone on a trip, been arrested, gotten married? Had she renounced her habit? No one ever found out. But for Lily, as for Marie-Jacqueline, her memory was tied up with that of the two deceased women.

Both of them, moreover, were in the grip of their own destinies, which were leading them hastily along toward the conclusion of their lives. Marie-Jacqueline had come seeking asylum with Lily, who'd accepted her plea wholeheartedly. But the pair of women weren't unaffected by conflict. Lily had no qualms about treating her friend as a maid. She gave her tedious errands and forced her to put up with a consistently bad mood.

Moreover, Marie-Jacqueline wasn't the most tactful of guests. She added her disorder to Lily's, taking her clothes, using her powder and makeup. Arguments flared up over a hand towel or a toothbrush. But though they endlessly threatened to leave one another, they remained no less bound to one another through habit.

This is a common type of relationship, one that's all the more durable when the people brought together seem incapable of living harmoniously with one another. Because, in reality, both parties only have one true enemy: loneliness. They fear it, and they're haunted by a fear of the boredom and melancholy that comes with it, preferring confrontations and annoyance. There comes a day, however, when life sees to it that these hostile pairings come to an end. Each one then brags about having put an end to an unbearable state of affairs and puts full blame on the other for the inevitable rupture.

In this case, it was Marie-Jacqueline who took the initiative. Lily had been gone for several days. When she came back she found the house empty, her wardrobe and drawers pillaged: her linens, her furs, her jewelry were gone.

The concierge informed her that Marie-Jacqueline had left the day before, taking two large suitcases and not mentioning where she was going.

Lily discovered, in the days that followed, that she'd also ran up numerous debts with dealers, that she'd borrowed drugs from most of her friends.

Where she was, no one knew, no one ever would know.

Owing to the interest it aroused in her social circle, Lily ultimately derived more satisfaction than annoyance out of the robbery.

She played the role of the victim until the day it was clear that the story had lost its novelty. Marie-Jacqueline in turn moved into the realm of memories and allusions. She was out of the picture from then on. A rumor spread that she'd met her end, overcome with tuberculosis, in a sanatorium. It was entirely plausible.

There are days in Paris when the crowds are a forest of unknown faces. Then there are days when you run into someone you know around every corner. It can even seem as if all you need to do is think of someone to make them materialize. At place de l'Opéra, Barbara, bathed by sunlight and a warm breeze, saw Antoine. She went toward him, but the very moment she was about to place her hand on his shoulder, realized she was mistaken, that it wasn't Antoine but a stranger who didn't look anything like him. She hadn't even reached rue Scribe when she saw Antoine coming toward her. There was no doubt that it was him this time. The two of them then saw Auportain come out from Trou dans le Mur, the boulevard's marvelous little bar, and the three of them walked toward La Madeleine together. In front of les Trois Quartiers, Barbara pointed out a small surly looking woman.

"Arichetti's mother . . . ," she said.

These encounters, even the one with that ghostly woman, embellished the day. They came to a stop at the terrace at Weber. Long lines of cars, periodically stopped by the traffic lights, streamed by. From a taxi, a woman waved to them.

"It's Marie-Jacqueline," said Antoine.

"No . . . I don't think so . . . it's Lily," Barbara responded.

“Let’s agree that it’s Marie-Jacqueline wearing one of the dresses she stole from Lily.”

The procession of hours—accompanied by the sound of clocks not always in agreement, the noise of car engines and factories, by cigarette smoke—went on through the city, following the very rhythm of the blood pulsing through the veins of millions and millions of men throughout the world.

All three were vaguely aware of this erosion to the universe, of this projection of energy across unknown spaces, and, perhaps, they imagined the planet’s progression across horrifying distances, through new regions of the sky where fate had led it.

The lovely afternoon was characterized by the very melancholy of the sun. A languor was spreading through them. They decided to part ways, and Barbara took a taxi back home. At the roundabout on Champs-Élysées, the car got caught up in a traffic jam. She lifted her head and, in another taxi, stopped besides hers, she saw Courvoisier. They spoke briefly, but traffic began moving again and, as she went along avenue Montaigne toward place de l’Alma, Courvoisier headed toward l’Étoile.

This series of encounters had pushed her heart and mind into the depths of her memory. She recalled the happy days, the days of gatherings, when she could find pleasure in wearing a new dress, in showing up at Longchamp, at Deauville, or at a theater radiant with a beauty still adorned with the inimitable jewels of youth. Her taxi was following the Seine. She decided to redirect the driver to the little bistro where she’d wound up, one morning, with Antoine. It was empty. The regulars, for the most part workers, were laboring away in the factories. The proprietor was sleeping between the exhaustion of the morning and the evening rushes. The only customers were a housemaid knitting and a young boy diligently doing his homework at a small table. After being served, Barbara felt herself sink into an impalpable space that cut her off from the rest of world, which now seemed to her illusory and distorted, the way a fish must see it through the glass of an aquarium. Sounds didn't reach her, it seemed, without first undergoing a transformation that stripped them of their meaning. Was she alive? Was she truly Barbara? And this prison that'd suddenly been revealed to her, hadn't she been shut away in it for months and years? In the very heart of Paris, she felt exiled, more distant from civilization than she would have had she been lost within an unexplored continent. She could remember having seen Dondlinger here. He had left as well, like so many others, and, at that moment, she was the only person in the world thinking about him. She went home on foot. The Seine, in no rush to leave Paris, flowed toward bucolic landscapes, toward charming little towns where anonymous villagers bustled about in obscurity, toward the ocean where any evidence that it'd once been a river mirroring the fleeting scenes of the world would be lost. There, face to face with the sky, the anonymous and shapeless water would be lost in its reflection of the anonymous and shapeless sky, itself lost in passivity.

Each step that brought her closer to home seemed to immediately ring out in a past more remote than that of her most distant ancestors, prehistoric men and women living in caves and jungles, as distant as the very origin of all origins, at the bottom of matter's abyss.

Her pulse beat steadily. The store windows still reflected an attractive image. But a quiet despair had come over her. Never before had she experienced such distress, the metaphysical influence of which she was unaware. She attributed her need for opium to this spiritual disturbance, this sentimental disintegration. She straightened her posture, picked up her pace, hoping, through a vivacious demeanor, to force back the sense of death she felt inside her.

As soon as she was back home, she lit the lamp and prepared her pipe. The first puffs, however, did nothing to dispel her pain. Indeed, to the contrary, it only seemed to grow stronger. Her surroundings appeared to expand while she, in turn, was reduced to nothing more than an atom, lost in the body of a large, mysterious being endowed with an incredible amount of willpower and whose actions had become inscrutable. Thousands of kilometers separated her from her bedroom mirror, in the depths of which hurried thousands and thousands of faces she could will to appear. At the same time, she was painfully aware of the movements of her body: the rustling of air as it entered her lungs, her blood's journey through her veins, arteries, and heart, the quivering of her stomach and intestines, the functioning of her liver. Even her thoughts, which now seemed concrete and whose formation she could follow through the folds of her brain, and her bodily sensations, the transmission of which she could follow through her nerves.

No: tonight, opium wouldn't save her from her waking nightmare, which was causing her to suffer in both body and mind from an all-encompassing itch. She thought of the large bag of heroin she'd stored away in a drawer. She turned on the light after an almost insurmountable effort, not a physical effort but one of will, of decisiveness. She found the heroin and began to repeat its chemical name as if it were a refrain: diacetylmorphine hydrochloride, diacetylmorphine hydrochloride . . . there were almost five grams. She dissolved them into the smallest amount of water possible, which she then used to fill a ten-cubic-centimeter syringe.

"I'll just take a cubic centimeter and leave the rest."

She put the needle into her thigh and, in single movement, pushed the whole solution into her flesh, causing a large bump to form. She switched off the light and lay down in the darkness.

From that moment forward, there was nothing more than a body in the darkness, a body, deprived of feeling but not of movement, growing cold at the extremities. A soft and even death rattle sounded out. Fetid breath filled the room, whose curtains allowed the lights of the city and the passing cars to filter in. A horn sometimes drowned out the moribund voice and the tick-tock of the clock. The telephone rang several times. Some friend was waiting at one end of the electric wires that connected the city.

But Barbara could no longer hear, would never hear again.

A blanket slid onto the floor. The elevator came to a stop at the landing. The doorbell rang, then the sound of steps faded down the staircase.

Barbara could no longer hear, would never hear again.

Little by little her movements became less frequent, then stopped. The death rattle and interior noises of an organism struggling against decomposition stopped as well. Silence and darkness now reigned alone as masters of the apartment.

The next day, the sunlight, along with the usual daily noises, barely penetrated the bedroom. Then came night, then again the sun.

The cleaning woman discovered the corpse at around ten in the morning.

Barbara's death scattered the group of friends still a little more. They were no different than any other group of people spontaneously brought together by a vice, or, more simply, a common interest.

Chance brings them together and chance divides them. In groups of addicts, death, misfortune, and changes of household play larger roles than in any other. They're seasonal gatherings, if, that is, you allow the word season a broader meaning, one that conforms to the dimensions of life. First the poorest find themselves isolated, then the men who came only because of their unspoken love for Barbara. Courvoisier, Columot, and Antoine might have gone on seeing each other. But the first two, because of drugs, had troubles with money. As for Antoine, Barbara's death felt like a blow aimed directly at him. He blamed himself, during nights of insomnia, for the death he'd wished for. Her disappearance had, for him, though he wasn't quite aware of it, the humbling effect of a personal failure. He would at those moments regret not having known how to free her from her prison of smoke, for having been an accomplice in her suicide, a companion to her downfall. For the first time, the young man had doubts about his fate and morality. This remorse mixed with the dismay of not knowing where to spend his evenings. It wasn't that he was suffering from not smoking. But even if he wasn't addicted, he'd taken a liking to those fragrant hours, to the sentimental conversations. They'd filled up his free time, allowed him to lose contact with the real world, which he now faced once again, apart from the hours spent at work, with such timidity! Everything seemed bleak, hostile, gray. Without consciously doing so, he made a pilgrimage to the places he and Barbara had gone, the New-York Bar, the bistro of the Vel' d'Hiv', the Seine, this music hall, that restaurant. And each time the same eternal reproaches sounded inside him: "You should have saved her." "You could have saved her." "You wanted her to die." He was cleverly intoxicating himself with a pain more artificial than the paradises he'd known. Like a fetishist, he welcomed the most insignificant memories of the dead woman and sang to himself, day and night, a dirge in her honor. He considered suicide. But even if the thought took on a degree of familiarity, it wasn't sincere. Not that he particularly loved life. But life loved him. It possessed him. It pushed him to work and, through work, protected him from the drug. Thanks to work, thanks to life, there'd been evenings when, staggering with exhaustion, he'd gone home to sleep. And sleep was more imperative than either opium or love. He'd throw himself into bed, without eating, for twelve hours of darkness and dreams. The sleep, the darkness, the dreams had been beneficial interludes. Thanks to them, the drug had no authority over him. It was his servant, and the master didn't know just how lucky he really was. When he grew older, recalling the years of his youth and thus the years of dissipation, he would be able to speak about strength of character, of willpower, of temperament. Lies. He'd been nothing more than the privileged extra in a tragedy, the actor unwittingly cast in the best role who, in the final act, is tasked with enumerating the names of the dead.

But still, he must have somehow been aware of all this, because he vowed a personal hatred for opium, for heroin, for all narcotics. Not that he'd become afraid. From time to time, he again found himself holding a bamboo pipe or snorting a line of powder . . . He remembered:

"Do you want some?" Barbara had once said, holding out the packet and nail file toward him.

He smoked a dozen or so pipes, snorted two or three times, then refused to continue. Stopping required no effort on his part. Drugs bored him, and besides, with the exception of his desire for fortune and fame, however vague it was, no great body of work occupied his time, no ambition directed his actions.

Little by little, he rediscovered the outside world, the streets, life. He got used to seeing men he'd once looked down upon and was moved to discover that they were men and human beings. He surprised himself by taking an interest in shows, in games, and in studies, which the secret society of drugs had proscribed. He was surprised, even more so, to find inside himself a desire for women who didn't remind him of Barbara.

Slowly the remorse he felt for her faded, his memories of her grew more and more gentle. The old pain became pleasant to reawaken. The tears he shed in her honor were hot but sweet. Without any outward appearances of it, Antoine had grown older. He'd passed a landing on the staircase of age. He'd become a man. He was surprised to find himself speaking to younger people with an authority he'd been unaware of. He was surprised even more by the ease with which he went about his work and his ability to feel content. All the same, Barbara's ghost was there, present, imperious, a source of pain. Months went by.

Then one morning, the sun cold and the sidewalk dry, Antoine woke up, freed from his vain scruples and his old sorrows. Love and pain had crystallized. Maybe they'd left two wrinkles on his forehead or the first white hairs at his temples? The world again seemed vast and lively and worthy of being experienced. Barbara was now little more than a memory, though an unforgettable memory that would, through the progression of years, return to demonstrate its strength.

Antoine was not at all surprised when Courvoisier came by to offer him drugs. And Courvoisier was not at all surprised by Antoine's refusal. The distance between them had grown too large for them not to view each other with some sense of unfairness. Antoine had been unfair, Courvoisier as well. Antoine had stopped taking drugs. We've already seen that his taste for them was intertwined with Barbara. He refused. Courvoisier immediately assumed that he either had reserves or someone else to supply him, and he scolded himself for having once given him several dealers' addresses.

Running low on money, his only way to procure drugs now was through drugs themselves. That is to say: he'd begun selling them, he'd become a dealer himself. Moreover, he cheated his clients more than other dealers, because he knew how demanding need is and how easily, in case of shortage, an addict can satisfy himself with an adulterated powder, cut with sodium bicarbonate or bismuth. Auportain declined as well, but gave him the addresses of some potential clients. Auportain had an easy excuse. He only took opium and had a supply that could last several years. Then several months later, Columot forbade himself from using. His stupor was visible and Courvoisier, in comparison, still looked like a young man.

Besides several rare clients, Courvoisier was thus forced to rely on his acquaintance with women from Montmartre and Montparnasse, who bought their heroin by the gram. He was fully aware that this was the fastest way to fall into the hands of the police, or rather to be sacrificed by them. From now on, no one could come to his rescue if things turned dangerous. He was simply an inconsequential piece of the story, a name to give to journalists should they find themselves in need of it. Among his clients, how many would refuse to give his name on the mathematically inevitable day they found themselves compromised? How many of them were informants? How many would become one, voluntarily or out of fear? But, shackled to his physical need and driven on by danger and his need for money, he didn't stop.

He had to maintain professional relationships, to keep up with colleagues from the world of drugs, to do them favors and ask for them in return, to be their friend and to observe the strict rules of a profession that had its own set of laws, its own courts, speculators, capitalists, commoners, and aristocracy. Penalties await those who don't play by the rules, penalties that range from fines to execution, with denunciation to the police falling somewhere in between.

He aroused suspicion less through his acquaintances and transactions than through his appearance. His fear of the police was twice that of others. He was less afraid of personal degradation than the suffering he'd experience in prison as a dealer and an addict. And this fear ended up wreaking havoc on his face, warping his movements and his voice, transforming his vocabulary.

But his terror had to compete with his temerity, a propensity for the worst outcomes, an obscure desire for catastrophe. He successfully undertook insane schemes, such as, for instance, smuggling heroin to a client in prison. He briefly considered using Estival to bribe a guard. He decided not to. Instead, he hung about in bars frequented by guards, bribed one of them, had the drugs delivered.

This arrangement didn't last long. The guard was soon arrested. Courvoisier hid for several days. A waste of time. He hadn't been denounced, and his accomplice hadn't, for want of suspicion, asked for Courvoisier's name, meaning he alone bore the consequences of the crime.

But Courvoisier wasn't naïve enough to be completely put at ease by his impunity. His imprisoned client knew his name, and other dealers knew that he'd been supplying him. He had little hope of being definitively forgotten and suspected that they were waiting to use him when a more promising opportunity came along. Moreover, he had another reason to be worried. The whole affair had led to a lot of talk in the papers, in the circles of opium addicts and the confabs of dealers. He was afraid of becoming seen as suspect, of them attributing his tranquil demeanor to a relationship with the police. Suspected of being a rat, he knew that, one or way another, and without any hesitation, he'd be killed. He was far too insignificant a dealer to dare count on both the law and the world of criminals.

The Columot factory surprised Uncle Mazurier. Of modest means, he'd always imagined the theater of his nephew's activity as a black fortress, smoky and foreboding. But upon arriving he discovered no brick chimney rising up like a giraffe's neck, no slagheap, no workers waiting around a corner to rob him. All his ideas regarding Columot's work were turned upside down, ideas that had been vague to begin with, clichés derived from reactionary propaganda.

Geraniums grew in the courtyard. Stylish and attractive female employees strolled by. The men were cheerful and reminded him of his friends, of the people he knew in the far-off provincial town where he lived. They were neither downtrodden nor hostile. He surmised, thinking over the distressed telegram that'd asked him to come, that Columot didn't know how to handle his employees and that it was because of them that his situation had taken a turn for the worse. In this regard he was mistaken, as his nephew knew full well how to protect his money from the wage earners, perhaps even too well. Was he not the nephew of Columot the storekeeper, whose firm heart was legendary among his family and colleagues?

No, the factory was nice because its purpose—Columot made beauty products—allowed, demanded even, it to be so. The products had to be well presented, likewise the factory. It was necessary for the clientele. The personnel were clean and happy, somewhat owing to chance, mostly owing to their professional obligations.

As soon as Columot was with his uncle, he wasted no time with small talk. The presence of a family member, of his mother's brother, immediately softened him. He bemused the kind man with a jumbled recounting of his life as an addict and his problems as a businessman. His financial situation wasn't hopeless. But it was in jeopardy. They were doing their best to get it back in order, but he needed a relative to help him keep his peace of mind, to stand in for him, together with a carefully chosen lawyer, before the investors, while he went away to receive treatment. As far as that went, nothing to be concerned about. In a burst of lucidity he'd meticulously arranged his plans for recovery. But, with the exception of Mazurier, he couldn't trust anyone. He believed his uncle to be both incapable of wronging him and suspicious enough to not let himself get fooled. His manager and lawyer would advise the old man, who would in turn check their advice with another man of law. And Mazurier would earn a sum, a small sum that all the same shocked him, as if he'd been declared the winner of a jackpot. As for Columot, he'd go get treatment in the countryside. Mazurier, however, didn't immediately accept the offer. He asked for a day to think it over. After leaving his nephew, he took himself to the restaurant that, as a lonely bachelor and lover of food, he'd often spent nights dreaming of, chez Lapérouse. From his table he watched through the window a peaceful scene in which the Seine flowed imperceptibly, in which stood the Palais de Justice, reminding him of complicated stories involving notaries, attorneys, bailiffs, lawyers, long days spent on polished benches. He could make out, further on, place Saint-Michel and the setting of his commonplace but golden youth . . . the girlfriends, the nights of drinking.

He allowed the headwaiter to select his food and wine, and was subsequently served the kind of lunch he loved, with the spiced dishes balanced by more subtle and delicate ones, with sherry and Meursault wine supplying a drinkable source of sunshine.

As he ate and drank, the old man was once again experiencing the enthusiasm of his thirtieth year, when the death of his brother-in-law, Columot the storekeeper, had brought him face to face with a set of extremely difficult problems and dragged him into a crime drama whose details he preferred, for the sake of his digestion, not to think about. After he'd finished his meal, had his coffee, savored his brandy, he went to telephone Dr. Despére.

Despére, now a well-known practitioner, was an old friend from his years as a student, whom he'd seen with some regularity over the years. He'd become a great doctor, a wealthy healer, a member of the Academy of Medicine, and a founder, moreover, of a dynasty comprising his four sons, each one of whom had had great success on their *internat* exam and in their respective hospitals. At the other end of the line he heard the reassuring voice of his friend, that voice whose owner often claimed was, with the robustness and obvious health it expressed, partly responsible, along with science, for the success of his treatments. The cordial voice said that Mazurier was more than welcome to come over, grew worried when he mentioned a consultation, relaxed when he said it wasn't for himself.

Fifteen minutes later, Mazurier was in a taxi going to Despére's home on boulevard Malesherbes. Crossing the Pont Neuf, he thought about himself and his own health. The bridge suddenly seemed symbolic of his role. There was a difficult situation to be traversed. And Mazurier, as sturdy as the Pont Neuf, would help his nephew safely cross it, his scamp of a nephew whose youth, feats, and vices—and luck for having an uncle such as himself—he, without quite being able to admit it to himself, envied.

"My dear Mazurier, I don't know anything about drugs. And I don't care to know anything about them."

Mazurier raised his head to look Dr. Despére in the eye.

"You don't know anything? Well, this is certainly the first time I've heard you say anything like that."

"Listen. I've dealt with drug addicts before, but I'm done with all that. I don't want to hear anymore about them. When one comes to me I send him to the clinic. He could be on the verge of croaking and still I would refuse to look after him. It's not out of malice. But addicts, whoever they might be, are ingrates, cowards, and liars."

"Despére! We're talking about my nephew here, who's proven he's no coward!"

"That may be so. But you're here for a consultation, and I'm speaking to you with the frankness one owes a friend and a client. Here's how it goes. An addict arrives. He tells you all about how much he's suffered. He asks for drugs. You give in to pity. Then you examine him. The heart's not in great shape. The overall state of the body, the nerves, everything's a mess. You write him a prescription for heroin or morphine. Then he dies, and off you go to court. Or else he lives and you get a certain reputation . . . until the day you refuse. Then he drags your name through the mud everywhere he goes. Or he sends all the smokers and snorters in Paris your way. It always ends badly . . . the least of it is that he doesn't pay you. I had a friend I interned with, a splendid fellow, Fraille . . . his story's the same. He would see addicts. One of them got arrested and denounced him as a dealer. The newspapers got involved, as always, without any regard for the real story. The result: six months in prison and a five-year ban from practicing medicine. He's living out his life I don't know where, in some hole, finished, hopeless. I know another one who had some half-crazy woman die in his office ... after a shot of opium extract."

"But my God! I'm not asking you to look after him. I'm consulting you, asking you for advice. Give me some. You know me. I can save my nephew."

"And so, try ... I can promise you a wonderful outcome and a big payment of ingratitude ... If you want, go on my behalf to the Thaureau clinic in Mantes. It's the most dependable. They don't deal with anything else. But I can't guarantee you anything."

Mazurier stood up.

"How much do I owe you?"

"Don't be an old fool!" answered Despére. "Come to dinner this evening ... but don't bring your nephew ... I don't want to see him. Keep your money, but under one condition ... Keep me updated on how things unfold."

Mazurier couldn't restrain himself.

"I come to ask you for one little favor ... I was expecting more. There are worse things he could be doing than snorting that trash."

"There are indeed worse things, but it's still a very, very serious illness. Ah! If only your nephew was tubercular instead of an addict!"

"Is it really that bad? Why in God's name did they invent such poison?"

"The people who created it didn't know. They thought they'd found a morphine salt that wasn't intoxicating, you understand ... and that was much more effective. They were wrong, and then of course they didn't invent it for neurotics, they invented it for the truly ill, people who were suffering . . ."

"But my nephew is suffering, he has an illness . . ."

"No doubt he did. But his was a case that ought to have been dealt with by psychiatrists. If he were someone else I'd send him to Henri-Rousselle. But they're overburdened, and then he wouldn't have an easy time with the way things work there. He's not the place's usual patient. Trust me, go to Thaureau. Leave him there, by force if necessary, and when he leaves, don't let him out of your sight straightaway. Anyway, we'll talk about this again. In the meantime, come have dinner this evening, I have a Pommard in the cellar that you won't believe."

Mazurier came back late in the evening. He was in a good mood. He looked over the cozy dining room, the white tablecloth, the glassware, tableware, silverware. The smell of food came wafting out from the kitchen. He let out a sigh of contentment. His eyes went from Mme Despére to her four sons, each one strong and cheerful, then to Despére himself, who was also in a good mood thanks to the presence of his old friend. He'd been afraid that he'd offended Mazurier and had been worried by his late arrival.

"It's done," said Mazurier, "he's in Mantes. He went as easily as a child."

"That's good," said Despére, as he sunk a small spoon into a sea urchin. "May everything turn out as you hope. In any case, I'm as concerned with the matter as you are."

The social ruin of Courvoisier came shortly after his moral degradation. The two reinforced one another. Idleness is costly for someone who isn't accustomed to destitution. So as to preserve some appearance of wealth, he had to renounce life's genuine satisfactions, leaving his house for a hotel, selling his car. Drugs, American cigarettes, several repairs to his suit exhausted the last of his funds. He soon had to give up any pretense of dressing elegantly. His clothes marked him more clearly than a label. He was attractive; his appearance became dubious. He was seen with people whose presence he seemed to tolerate more than enjoy. People soon assumed that his intention was to get invited to smoking sessions so as to be able to borrow money from someone to pay his rent. This lowering of social standing, however, didn't take place from one day to the next. Each time he gave something up in order to have more money, Courvoisier rediscovered for several days, several weeks, his prestige, his carefree attitude, his generosity. He would then see his old friends, who could discern no change in him. If a cheap jewel had replaced a more expensive one, it was at least a good find from an antique shop, an object that, thanks to his taste, imparted a glimmer to his social twilight.

What had Courvoisier's sentimental life been up until that point? Attractive, wealthy, young, he hadn't yet found an opportunity for profound love. Or, rather, he'd been able to transfer this desire onto Barbara, whose fate he'd intuitively expected. It was already a dead woman he'd loved in her, a presence that had extinguished all his appetite, all his passion. It'd conformed to the knowledge that every man has of his own destiny. He'd loved her, a future corpse, a corpse-to-be, because he'd considered himself a corpse-to-be. Less finesse would have bestowed upon him—in addition to the heaviness essential to bronze statues—balance and severity, the virtues of tightrope walkers, poets, and philosophers. Reason spoke to him, but if he didn't speak back it was out of weakness, and he preferred to run away from it in search of an impossible form of madness, a madness that was little more than a disguise. He looked down on Columot, Antoine, Auportain. They astonished him, but he forbade himself from admiring them. Their company became as intolerable to him as his was for them, but he was still unable to erase them from his memory. He thought of them often and sometimes forced himself to visit them. He then convinced himself without almost any hesitation that what he had to say was of scant importance to them. He could calculate the extent of his downfall based on the coldness, ever increasing, with which they greeted him. But he couldn't be angry with them, or reproach them for their ingratitude. It wasn't the Courvoisier they'd known that they were rejecting, it was a Courvoisier who'd become a barely recognizable caricature of himself that they wanted to prevent from interfering with their memories of happier years.

Their friendship had come about because of a shared insouciance.

But Auportain had never renounced his selfish withdrawal, his pleasant, drawn-out death.

And Antoine was discovering the world and the seasons and the joys of a life free of any fog or haze.

And each day Columot was more efficiently killing the beautiful archangel he'd once been.

Courvoisier experienced evenings characterized by a morose emptiness, a solitude that his spiritual indigence could do nothing to protect him from. He grew accustomed to cafés where people stay until closing, to shallow conversations, to acquaintances not only dubious, which hardly would have mattered, but stupid as well.

And soon he gave himself up to a fate whose end, had he not been so cowardly, he would have been able to foresee.

Meanwhile, scientific instruments he'd once used were entrusted to others. Younger people discarded his favorite scale. Life went on without him. He was visible but absent.

Dondlinger had found at Henri-Rousselle a sense of peace and salutary isolation. But things were different for Columot at the rest home in Mantes. His nerves collapsed and he was at first a quarrelsome, inattentive, idiotic wreck incapable of responding to the questions asked of him.

The worst thing about it was his own awareness of his behavior.

"I'm going senile," he would repeat to himself.

They employed, to begin with, a slow detoxification method. He had extreme difficulties until the day he bribed his nurse to get him heroin, which was rather expensive but of an unexpected quality. He then regained his vitality and cheerfulness. But Dr. Thaureau's was a strict establishment. The secret of this unusual recovery was soon discovered, and the nurse was fired after a rebuke that convinced him to go looking for a career that doesn't require a conscience.

Despére had telephoned on his behalf.

"I refused, out of principle, his uncle's request to look after him. But it's very important to me that his treatment is successful. Think of him as my relative. If something's not going well, let me know about it."

Having learned about the smuggled heroin, he agreed with his fellow doctor that a rapid detoxification using Démorphène would be best. Supervision of the patient was increased, as it wasn't only necessary to give the treatment with precision but also to protect him from possible mishaps.

Columot was thus treated more or less like the patients at Henri-Rousselle, although his injections were weaker and given with greater frequently. Night and day he was visited, observed, looked after. His mood, once again foul, gave way when confronted with the doctor's composure. Moreover, the promise of finishing sooner aroused his hope. He was too lucid not to notice the sick person who dwelled inside of him. One day, he gave the nurse several books he'd brought with him, the sight of which alone now bothered him: *Opium Smokers* and *Opium Smoke*, both of which now seemed exceedingly silly. On the other hand, he was unable to give up *Artificial Paradises* by Baudelaire, whose moral, which had always escaped him, which he hadn't wanted to absorb, was now making itself more evident by the day.

But his blindness was excusable. Like his friends, he'd only wanted to read the parts of the book that stroked his pride. Baudelaire, De Quincey: these were prestigious names. He and his friends could boast about being their brothers through opium, though it was a brotherhood less prestigious than any other.

Forced to face himself, Columot saw little more than a landscape littered with ruins. The battles he'd waged had all ended in defeat. He was surprised to suddenly find himself, with his fortieth birthday approaching, counting the failures of the handsome, heroic adolescent he'd once been. He didn't dare admit to himself that he was afraid of getting older and that through drugs he'd hoped to find a potion for eternal youth. He was nostalgic for the time when his mistresses had also been mothers, when his reputation had sufficed to bring him beautiful, quivering bodies who were less interested in his heart and spirit than in his budding virility and the glory of the battles he'd taken part in.

Where was the Columot of 1918, the breaker of plates and glasses, the terrible, spoiled child whose Croix de Guerre and its numerous palms had been enough to excuse his follies in the eyes of even the strictest individuals, in the same way that one overlooks the tantrums of the dying. He'd been unable to accept the end of the war. He'd continued it without realizing that the dangers he faced as a civilian were crueler and more precise than those that threaten the fighter pilot. And so, as a man, he'd behaved like an overgrown child, been cradled like an infant, and obeyed orders that were by all appearances absurd.

The hours passed slowly. His rediscovery of time's true duration comforted him. The clouds, whose course he followed from his window, always went by too quickly.

Eventually, he came to fear leaving what had become a refuge, and only Uncle Mazurier—slow witted, narrow minded, shut off from the higher forms of thinking—could reassure him. The tenderness he felt for Mazurier was comforting in the same way a simple, flavorful dish is when offered without pretension in a modest setting. The old man's heart was naïve, but his reliability gave Columot hope. He now dreamed of an obscure life in a provincial town, of work without glory, of simple, commonplace pleasures. He fearfully considered the day when he'd again find himself responsible for his own well-being, burdened by the intimidating task of finding new habits. He casually wondered if he'd go back to the pipe, the tray, and the little oil lamp, which shone in his memory like a night-light at the end of an inescapable corridor. He couldn't hide from himself the fact that his life had been aimless and hollow since the day he'd ceased being a soldier, ceased receiving orders from which he could at least derive the rare pleasure of disobedience. He'd believed himself to be a senior officer. He was nothing more than a subaltern. His puerile lifestyle had dulled, because he'd lacked some peremptory ambition, everything of value inside him. He imagined the possibility of marrying a sweet and dutiful woman but was afraid of giving her his anxieties and instability as dowry.

He didn't interact with the other patients and even avoided them when he was allowed to walk though the clinic's park, strolling about in a solitary dream, disappointed to find himself mostly indifferent to the summertime landscape.

The sun itself was a star without connotation, dead, artificial, and destined, it seemed, to roll from one wall to another in an abandoned cemetery, where on the deteriorating graves he could make out familiar names that evoked neither beloved faces nor recognizable voices.

Detoxification had led him into a deserted world, one without shelter, without hours, without seasons, with neither day nor night.

Uncle Mazurier came regularly to visit his nephew during his two-month stay at the clinic. He updated him on the business, pretended to give him a comprehensive account of its operations, and urged him to share his thoughts. By doing so, the kind man hoped to help the patient rediscover an interest in his company. He himself couldn't imagine anything else in existence worthy of so much concern and passion. There was something in Columot that puzzled him. What could he have been looking for in drugs? What kind of sensations did they have to offer him? He imagined indescribable pleasures and, if he'd had the courage, he would have asked, just once, to sample the magic powder or the resin of illusions. But he did nothing of the sort. His sensual indulgences were limited to top-quality food and top-class wines.

And so, when Columot was released by the doctor, Mazurier took him on a trip through Burgundy, covering Joigny and Beaune, Auxerre and Dijon, Arnay-le-Duc and Villefranche-sur-Saône. He hoped to reconcile his nephew with the realities of life through large glasses of Pommard and Corton, with the help of quenelles, escargots, roasts a la crème, feasts.

He didn't realize that his companion was only a shell of a person. Columot, incapable of resisting Mazurier, passively endured his uncle's presence, all the while longing for the moment he'd again be alone. He did feel a tender gratitude for him, but still, the chasm that separated them! There could be no meaningful exchange of confidences: one loved a life without splendor but loved that life fiercely, while the other asked for too much, because he hadn't obtained what he'd vaguely desired, and was contemplating suicide. Mazurier might have thought himself indulgent, but it was his nephew who truly embodied the word.

One evening, after a magnificent dinner in their hotel, Columot noticed shadows moving on the corridor's ceiling while he returned to his room. A soft light carved out the shadows of two hands, and he had no trouble recognizing the movements' purpose. He stopped a moment. He could smell the unforgettable fragrance of opium. He was about to knock, to beg for several pipes or a pellet. But the light went out and, disappointed, he went to lie down.

Back in Paris, he would sometimes smell it on the street. He would inhale the air with a tilt of the head and try to guess from which window it was escaping.

Uncle Mazurier soon left. Now that he considered his task complete, now that someone else was in charge of the factory, he was overcome with a longing to be back in Angoulême. Proud of himself, he went home, filled with love for the boy who'd given him a chance to be useful and to hold himself in slightly higher esteem.

Courvoisier smiled sadly as he looked over Antoine's accommodations.

"I can see Auportain's influence. It's a rather poetic idea to frame the first pages of the illustrated supplements in *Le Petit Journal.* Artists are still dawdling about with their Épinal prints . . . This assassination of President Carnot, that arrival by Barnum, this eruption of Vesuvius . . . those are real examples of popular modern art."

He suddenly stopped before a chromo that must have belonged to a calendar from the 1880s.

It depicted, beneath a stormy sky, an emaciated horse grazing on the scattered grass of an enclosed plot of land, in which bones were whitening on the ground. In the background, on a dreary house, was a sign that read: *Butcher*. Van Gogh had mentioned this chromo in a letter to his brother, recounting how much it had affected him when he first saw it on the wall of an inn.

Courvoisier looked it over thoroughly, and Antoine realized that several similarities existed between his friend and the horse. Like the animal, he'd bounded along with the wind of youth, a young stallion intoxicated by air and space and sky. Like the animal, he'd been a handsome, robust creature, proud of his strength and unconcerned about the passing of days, of seasons. And, as had happened with the animal, time had caught up with him. He seemed excessively skinny beneath his still stylish but nearly worn-out clothing. Deep shadows sat under his eyes. His thin nose looked unusually large. His face no longer suggested youth, but instead seemed mummified, wasted, the daylight cruelly revealing its true nature.

Courvoisier said:

"This is classic Auportain. Now here you have someone who understands and appreciates Van Gogh! But those … those are completely you."

And he pointed at the mantelpiece, upon which sat two or three nickel-plated toys, marvels of mechanics.

"We're not so far from our childhoods, you and me … no one is … not even Auportain. Those toys were probably made by paunchy men, workers, fathers, or, who knows, a brilliant former student from Polytechnique."

Antoine was getting dressed as he listened to Courvoisier. In his words, he heard a Courvoisier he'd thought had vanished and was feeling a renewed sense of affection for him. He'd put on a starched shirt, knotted a black tie, slipped into a pair of tuxedo pants. He was now buttoning his vest.

"Antoine," said Courvoisier, "I owe you a lot. Thanks to your good relations with the police …"

Antoine thought he could detect some malevolent intention in his voice. It was there. He felt it. A wave of bitterness rose in his heart. Courvoisier went on:

"Thanks to your good relations with police, I've avoided prison and who knows … worse, maybe. As painful as it is for me to do, I'm going to ask you for another favor. I'm an addict. You know that. For the love of everything we love, of everything we have loved . . . let me borrow two hundred francs."

"I'm not happy about this, Courvoisier . . . but fine . . ."

With a pang of compassion and sadness, Antoine recognized a wool tie around his friend's neck that he'd seen before, during his days of splendor. He was almost finished dressing.

"I don't mean to be a nuisance, but I'm in a bit of a rush. I barely have enough time to find the dealer. Do you mind if I have it now? We're old enough friends to be direct with one another."

"The problem is I don't have any change. I'll have to break a thousand."

"Give it to me . . . I'll get the change."

Antoine handed over the bill. Courvoisier took his hat. Just before going out the door, he turned around and went to get his raincoat.

"I think it's raining," he said flatly.

Antoine, ready to be on his way, smiled. He let him go without another word. The door slammed shut. Antoine took another bill from the drawer, got his hat and overcoat, and left quietly. He could hear Courvoisier rushing down the stairwell, then his hurried steps in the entrance hall. When he came out into the street, he saw him getting into a taxi at the corner.

Antoine smiled sadly.

"A thousand francs wasted. A friend lost . . . Oh, a friend!"

He lit a cigarette and walked to the bus stop. He noted its number; since a taxi was passing, he stopped it, gave the driver the address of a restaurant, and settled into a corner of the car.

Without drugs, Columot was like a man who's had a gland indispensable to the use of human faculties surgically removed. Both his life and the world at large seemed stripped of all interest, of all flavor. Moreover, he was undergoing a physical transformation. He was putting on weight. His body was developing a shapeless appearance that caused a component of his charm, which had come entirely from his stamina and vigor, to disappear. His hair began thinning. His expression lost its confidence. And this all was augmented by a disdain, a disgust, with clothing and fashion. He felt himself entering a definitive decline, more damaged from his short period of abstinence than from ten years of opium use. Or, perhaps, abstinence had suddenly brought previously hidden scars to the surface. He would most certainly have started smoking again if a fortuitous encounter hadn't made him change his social milieu and choice of vice. In a restaurant, he found himself seated beside a fat man whose face stirred some memory. The man, moreover, seemed as puzzled and intrigued as Columot was. They ended up speaking and realizing the source of their bemusement. It was Platard, a comrade from his squadron; Platard, whom he'd known when they were both young men, during the exhilaration of the war. It was a time in their lives that had blazed like an oil well. They reminisced over their battles and their nights of drunkenness, their mistresses and their follies, the cocaine, the alcohol, the long nights, the broken plates, the heroism. Stripped of their armor and good looks, and of no interest to anyone, they were now just two aging men nostalgic for the distant past. The war hadn't even bequeathed them some glorious story to pass on as a legend or in a song. Their memories made younger men yawn; the women they'd loved were old, overweight half-wits. The fortune that had once shined on them was a fortune made of paper money, from which they were incapable of drawing lasting joy. They were overcome with self-pity and drank to the point of stupor, just as they'd used to. Each wanted to prove to the other that he still had his former stamina. Their debauchery lasted a week and took them to places where, in the past, wearing their awe-inspiring uniforms, they'd reigned supreme, with all the glory becoming of their palm-adorned Croix de Guerres. Some clubs had disappeared; others had changed their style. They experienced a sentimental pain at no longer hearing the music of yesteryear, this song from 1917, that one from 1919. They demanded that the orchestra play: "J'ai un femme qu'adore les animaux"; "Ça c'est pour vous"; "Tu le reverras, Paname"; "Over there" or "Elle a un caractère en or," "Eléonore," and "Salut à la papa." They could reliably find at least one musician who remembered their request and who was then able to lead the rest of the orchestra. But the songs were never played the way they'd once been, and the two friends would sit in their corner trying to re-create the music that'd served as an accompaniment to their rowdier years.

Columot came out of the experience conquered by alcohol and definitively submissive to the demands of his life. To the great satisfaction of his uncle, who wasn't one to judge heavy dinners or excessive drinking, he went back to managing his factory. When Columot ran into a friend from his days of opium use, he was always surprised to discover the barriers of communication that had arisen between them. And he was surprised most of all to be so hurt by Barbara's absence. And yet he didn't think about her death; only her absence, an absence that was without reason, found a way into his thoughts. He enjoyed finding a detail on a woman's face that he'd once seen on Barbara's . . . the color of her hair, the shape of her eyes, the expression on her mouth, a familiar movement of a hand or body.

He grew used to frequenting card games in cafés, to returning home each evening in a mental fog that reminded him of opium, to joyless mornings, to unfulfilling work. He even found himself with more money than he knew how to spend. His physical transformation became more noticeable and no one would have been able to see within this overweight man, talking about stock prices and the latest aviation news, a pilot whose style had once been worthy of *Vie Parisienne*. He was Columot, well-to-do retailer, firmly established manufacturer, punctual with his payments, always on time to meetings, sharing all the received wisdom of his profession, someone who, according to his staff, loved the bottle and was in "good shape," using the phrase to simultaneously reference his physical fortitude and the state of his personal fortune.

Years later, in the fog of his memory, thoughts of Barbara's group blended with his feats during the war and the joys of his early childhood. There had been, before, a Columot for whom the surviving Columot would have been unable to vouch for. Nor would he have been able to reconstruct an accurate image of this missing individual, to imagine his thoughts, to relate his splendid times or the dangers he'd once experienced.

Why this day instead of any other? Why this specific time? Courvoisier asked himself the question as soon as he saw Estival on the sidewalk of boulevard de Courcelles. He was coming from rue de Prony with some sixty grams of heroin in his pockets. He didn't try to run away, even though Estival might not have tried to pursue him. The policeman came up to him and, without a word, walked at his side toward place des Ternes. They were about to cross rue Pierre-le-Grand, at the end of which shone the dome of the Russian church. The sight fixed itself in Courvoisier's mind and served as the accompanying image to his companion's first words:

"Mr. Courvoisier, don't resist. There's nothing I can do. I'm arresting you. Come with me to the station. I'm sorry, but I did warn you."

"Ah, don't be sorry. Do your job and let's not say another word about it."

At the station, Estival made a show of searching him. He took most of the packages but, no doubt intentionally, let him keep two grams.

They didn't lock him up. They left him at the station, on a bench. Several times, the prisoner asked to go to the bathroom. He was taken there with minimal supervision and was able to snort without disturbance. The day was reaching its end. The sun came in through the door, and the rectangle it was projecting onto the floor slowly changed shape.

Then came the night, during which the only distractions were the officers' card game, visits by men and women in search of some lost possession, the arrest of two or three noisy drunkards who sank quickly into sleep at the back of their cells. The sound of the automatic flushing systems could be heard at regular intervals coming from inside them.

Around two o'clock in the morning, two officers brought in a blood-covered man. What was the reason for his arrest? Courvoisier didn't understand. Nor was he particularly interested. The man was quiet and the two officers spoke about him in low voices. Then everyone, officers and detained, fell into a state of drowsiness in which the noises of the street and the sound of voices took on an uncanny timbre. Cars were passing more and more rarely outside.

Through this mental haze, Courvoisier perceived the unfolding of his destiny and gave himself up to it. Head in hands, half-dreaming, half-conscious, he stared at his shoes, the laces of which had been removed.

Now only the officers coming back from watch duty or going on it broke the night's monotony.

His shoes were the only things his mind was truly aware of. He looked over their wrinkles, their cracks. He counted the points where the leather was attached to the sole. They were gaping open because of all the empty eyelets and were now little more than sad objects on whose colored surfaces he could make out landscapes and faces. The brown here was turning to red, there to yellow, elsewhere to black. He watched a ridiculous dream unfold between the three latter colors, a dream of escape, a dream of intervention, a dream of invisibility. Sometimes he made a fleet-footed escape through the streets, sometimes Antoine and Columot came into the station, had him freed, led him away to end the night in a quiet brasserie where he was served delicious beer, strong-smelling sauerkraut, plump mussels. And sometimes he disappeared suddenly from the sight of the officers and of everyone else, then went to seek refuge inside some warm palace with soft carpets, where he lived unbeknownst to the inhabitants, listening to their secrets, eating their food, drinking their wine, sleeping on their couches, warming himself by their fires, a carefree witness to the events of their lives and to the events of the world. This anonymity reminded him of his childhood, the carefree games, the warmth of his mother's stomach before birth.

The chill morning air made him shiver. An officer came in with a large pot of coffee. They offered him a cup. He drank it while thinking back to mornings after a night of opium, now a part of the past, during a time when he'd been happy.

Suddenly, the sun reappeared, reflected by the windows of the house across the street, a pale sun, without sparkle, like a glass of champagne forgotten during the course of a party. He sighed. He felt a hand on his shoulder. Estival was standing before him.

"I wanted to spare you the police wagon. I have a car. Come on."

He gave him back his belt, his tie, his shoelaces, and they went out into the street. The inspector affected a friendly tone with him, but if someone familiar with such situations happened to pass by he would have been able to see through to the truth of the matter: that was most certainly a prisoner going by.

In the car, Estival put his arm around Courvoisier's shoulder and whispered in his ear:

"I can't not arrest you. They're going to question you. Listen to me. Do not admit to dealing drugs. Deny, deny! Just admit to using. Whatever the case, they're not going to be too hard on you."

And, with that, Courvoisier's hope was renewed.

No, the interrogators weren't too hard on him. Everything went quickly and the inspectors had spoken, though without deference, rather politely. Estival had surely talked to them in advance. But Courvoisier wondered why he hadn't been at the interrogation, why he seemed to have abandoned him. Truth be told, Estival was quite delighted to have nothing more to do with him. More than anything else, he feared that Antoine would come ask him to intervene on his friend's behalf, for whom he couldn't help but feel pity and sympathy.

Courvoisier's case was now a matter for the examining magistrate. He was happy at first to find himself alone in a cell, which allowed him to snort the rest of the drug in peace. But the solitude soon began to weigh on him. He obsessively considered his wasted, hopeless life. He knew full well that everything was over, that he was entering a new world, that nothing was left for him of his friendships, his connections, his habits, his intellectual and social circles.

He thought over his interrogation at the criminal investigation department and realized bitterly that, had the inspectors been more curious, he would have given them the names of all his clients, of all his friends, and of all the drug dealers he'd been involved with. He knew such a denouncement would have put him in serious danger, not to mention that the idea also disgusted him for purely moral reasons. Yet all strength of character had abandoned him at the very moment he'd promised himself to be at his most courageous. And he knew that, placed in similar circumstances, he would be just as cowardly, just as sapped of energy. He thus feared another appearance before the officers or the committing magistrate. His solitude, moreover, was taking a tighter hold of him just as the symptoms of withdrawal were beginning to kick in. He assumed it was out of self-interest that Estival had left him opium, in the hopes of making him confess everything he knew once deprivation had removed his last bit of pride.

He felt pain everywhere, and all at once. It made breathing torture, it gnawed away at his intestines, made even his bones, tendons, and veins feel impossibly sensitive. He began hallucinating and could no longer trust his senses. He thought he heard his name called. He thought he saw the door of his cell open. He could smell foul odors wafting around him. Nauseating flavors filled his mouth . . .

A guard came in and asked if he was sick. He thought it might be a trap and said no.

When he was alone again, he meticulously went through his pockets, gathering whatever dust could be found. He snorted it. It might have contained a bit of heroin, it might have been all in his head, but, either way, he felt relief. Short-lived relief.

A fear of death came over him. He began to moan softly. But, afraid of making the guard come back, afraid of being interrogated, afraid of being taken to the infirmary, he forced himself to keep quiet.

Suddenly, his eyes fastened upon the wall. Using his fingernails, he scratched off the plaster. He snorted it, and managed to find some satisfaction in the ersatz substitute.

He was sweating. Shudders ran up and down his body, and his skin was in a terrible state of irritation.

He took off his jacket and began to scratch himself violently, angrily. In his rage, he ripped his shirt. He took it off, tore it again until he had a small strip of cloth, which he then tied to the foot of the bed and passed his head through. Then, with a violent jerk, he strangled himself.

One April afternoon, Antoine ran into Auportain along the Seine in Auteuil. Auportain put his hand on the other's shoulder and led him into a café that put one in mind of Provence. A weak sun shone over the area. A tugboat passed pulling a line of barges. Cars drove quickly by. The embankment was nearly deserted. They could hear the shouts of children playing on the bank.

"How are things?"

"I'm working."

"What about the pipe?"

"The pipe? I'm finished with that. It doesn't interest me anymore."

"But you wouldn't say no to smoking one or two over at my place tonight, would you?"

"Tonight? Can't. I'm busy. How about tomorrow?"

"Can't. I'm leaving on the eight o'clock train for Cannes."

"Well, it'll have to be another time then."

"Are your plans tonight really so important?"

"No. Just some friends, old friends, who I promised to have dinner with. I wouldn't want them to be offended."

"And after dinner?"

"I'm taking them to the theater and then I'm going to bed. I have some work I need to take care of in the morning."

Auportain put his hand over Antoine's. A paternal smile, somewhat sad, lit up his face.

"You're saved, Antoine. Not abandoning something to go smoke a pipe, that says it all. Had you straight out refused me, I would have thought that you had your own supply back home and that you didn't want to put up with my company. But you also refused to put off plans that you yourself admitted were of little importance, you chose your old friends—and it seems to me you're seeing them not because you especially want to, but because you feel obliged to—over a night of opium. That's also a good sign. If we see each other again, Antoine, I won't ask you to smoke, but I do hope that today you'll do me the pleasure of dining with an old fellow whose life has become somewhat drab."

"Auportain . . ."

"Yes, you know, Barbara's death was very difficult for me. I would have liked to have saved her . . . I'm sorry, am I upsetting you?"

"I have something to say, too. Barbara's death affected me, deeply. It made me reconsider things, and now I wonder if I really loved her. If I loved her for her or for myself. I'm not at all sure that I really loved her . . . if I had I would have gotten her away from all that."

"When have you ever seen love without selfishness? You don't love for yourself, you don't love for others. You love a woman for her and also for yourself. Don't blame yourself for anything. It's not your fault. And whatever you do, don't follow my example. An experience similar to yours led me to give up on life. And I did give up. But I shouldn't have. Now I'm the old ghost in a sentimental cemetery . . . and in this past year I've seen quite a few people buried . . ."

"It's true . . . so many dead! Barbara, Berthe, Jeanne, Simonne Remige, Dondlinger, Artenac, Courvoisier, not to mention Arichetti, a walking corpse in that asylum . . ."

"All the same, you're here, before me, saved. I'm sure of it. There's not a doubt in my mind. And being with you gives me some consolation."

From a neighboring courtyard came the sound of clumsily played piano scales. It was four o'clock. Children on their way home from school passed by laughing and jostling one another. The two men watched them in silence. Then Auportain placed a bill on the table.

"Hope to see you again sometime soon, my dear Antoine."

And then he left.

Antoine Maison, filled with a melancholic joy, watched him go. He felt as if he held the universe in his heart, and never had the universe seemed so large.

Several months before the events that have just been recounted, Antoine found himself walking back toward Paris at dawn through the Bois de Boulogne. Between Suresnes and Saint-Cloud, he'd stayed late at the bargemen's parties and at the bistros, where people had been playing dice. Already he liked breaking away, alone, from his friends whose lives were beginning to seem more and more pitiful, their companionship more and more questionable.

He'd crossed the dark, glistening, bulging Seine. Lights moved about on board the barges. The sky was growing pale.

His mouth bitter from the alcohol and tobacco, he breathed in the cold air of the expiring night. The lights of Paris were growing indistinct with the approach of dawn. The woods were numb. The sonorous trot of a horse could be heard in the distance, which grew gradually louder until a milk carriage went speeding by him. Antoine walked along briskly and cheerfully, cleansed and refreshed by the morning air, happy to feel the life that was flowing through him.

The whiteness of the road stood out against its surroundings. In the dark copses, some animal, a lost dog or a runaway cat, rustled about. The beating of wings could be heard in a tree. Coming to the lakes, he heard a loud dive, then the lapping of water against the boats and the jingling of their chains.

A car was approaching. Its headlights were strong, the interior brightly lit. An impassive driver drove it slowly forward. The car was floating rather than rolling. Antoine, lost in his thoughts, ignored it.

A moment later, he heard it approaching again from behind him. The headlights lengthened the walker's shadow, then the car brushed by him. This time, he looked inside.

On white satin cushions, completely nude and with undone blond hair, rested a magnificent creature. The car continued along its way, turned around in the distance, and came back, even more slowly, to brush by him again. He went on walking while the car repeatedly performed this same maneuver. Each time it passed, Antoine looked over the beautiful white body, the indifferent face, the soft shadows that gave shape to the skin.

Finally, when the car brushed by him even closer still, he put a foot on the running board and reached for the door. In response to some command, the car took off at an extreme speed, almost knocking Antoine to the ground.

Now, it continued along the road. Antoine watched it shrink beneath the shadows of the trees, which it lit up, patch by patch, like a stage set. Then it turned onto a crossroad. On the surface of the road on which Antoine was walking, the shadows of tree trunks spun like the spokes of a giant wheel. Soon, the light could only be seen in distant flashes, and then at last disappeared completely.

Antoine arrived in Paris with the break of day. The trees were filled with the chirping of birds. A rooster crowed beside a gateman's house. People were moving about in the Val d'Or train station. Rows of workers were passing through the Porte Maillot. The pleasant smell of coffee came drifting out from the percolators in the first cafés to open on avenue de la Grande-Armée. The streetlights went out.

The die was cast . . .

Jesse L. Anderson is a writer and translator originally from Olympia, Washington. This is his fourth book-length translation from the French, and his translations of stories and articles have appeared in various publications, including *Vice*, *Conjunctions*, and the 2016 and 2018 editions of *Best European Fiction*. His debut novella, *The Western Contingent*, is published by Dalkey Archive Press.